J
CH

When the
Beginning Began

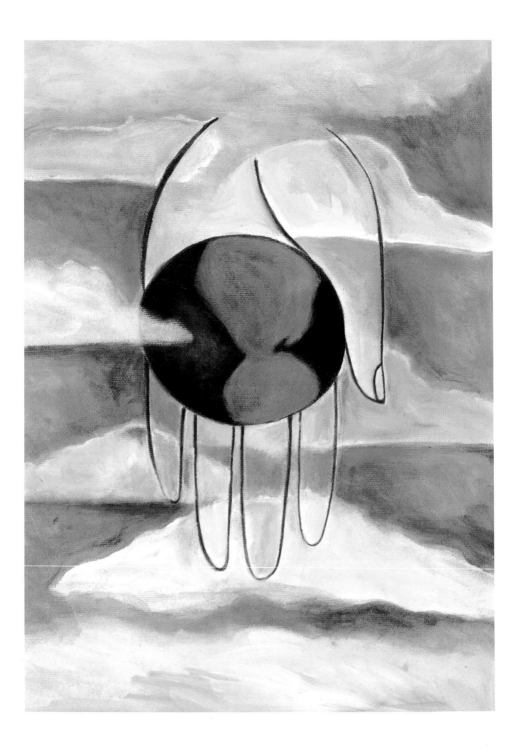

Julius Lester

When the Beginning Began

STORIES ABOUT GOD, THE CREATURES, AND US

Illustrations by EMILY LISKER

SILVER WHISTLE

HARCOURT BRACE & COMPANY

San Diego   New York   London

Ani l'dodi v' dodi li
I am my beloved's and my beloved is mine
To my wife, Milan

Text copyright © 1999 by Julius Lester
Illustrations copyright © 1999 by Emily Lisker

Library of Congress Cataloging-in-Publication Data
Lester, Julius.
When the beginning began: stories about God, the creatures, and us/by Julius Lester;
illustrated by Emily Lisker.
p.   cm.
"Silver Whistle."
Includes bibliographical references.
Summary: A collection of traditional and original Jewish tales interpreting the biblical story of the
creation of the world.
ISBN 0-15-201238-9
1. Creation—Juvenile literature.   2. Bible stories, English—O.T. Genesis.   3. Legends, Jewish.
[1. Creation.   2. Bible stories—O.T.   3. Jews—Folklore.   4. Folklore.]   I. Lisker, Emily, ill.
II. Title.
BS651.L39   1999
296.1'9—dc21   97-37352

Text set in Fairfield
Designed by Camilla Filancia
First edition   F E D C B A

Printed in Singapore

Contents

Introduction

There is a tradition in Judaism called midrash, a Hebrew word whose root means "to inquire, to investigate." Specifically, midrash refers to ways of interpreting a biblical text as well as the commentaries and stories that have come from this method of interpretation.

Biblical stories eschew details. They say only what is needed to tell the story. Throughout Jewish history, rabbis and laypeople have created midrashim (plural) to answer such questions, and they continue to do so today. (A fine example of contemporary midrashim is *Does God Have a Big Toe?* by Rabbi Marc Gellman.)

For some years I have taught a course at the University of Massachusetts called Biblical Tales and Legends, in which I lead students in studying some of the major stories in the book of Genesis and the traditional legends around them. When I began this book it was going to be a straightforward retelling of Jewish legends about God's creation of the world and its inhabitants. But something happened. Just as I find new meanings in the biblical stories every time I teach the course, when I sat down to write this volume, my imagination opened to the text in newer ways still.

What does it mean to use the imagination to explore a biblical text? An example: In Gen. 4:8, there are these words—"And Cain spoke to Abel his brother. And it came to pass, when they were in the field, that Cain rose up against Abel his brother, and killed him." The text tells us that Cain spoke to Abel. However, it does not tell us what Cain *said* to Abel. This is an opportunity—indeed, an invitation—for a midrash. What *did* Cain say? Did Abel respond? What is the relationship between what Cain said and the subsequent murder of his brother? Is there a relationship between what Abel said or did not say and Cain's killing him? The beauty of midrash is that there are almost as many answers, that is, stories, to the question as there are people who care to explore the text with sacredness.

For example, Judaism, as well as Christianity and Islam, posits that God is eternal. This means God existed before he created the world. So, what was he doing? Why did he stop whatever it was he was doing and create the world and all its inhabitants? I wanted answers to these questions, questions that Jews at other times might not even have dared ask. But today we do not accept very much, if anything, on faith. We want to know for ourselves. Where there is no possibility of arriving at a rationally definitive answer, we use our imagination because it can go where reason cannot.

As I began writing, what were to have been retellings of traditional midrashim quickly grew beyond their original boundaries. God and the angels acquired distinct personalities, and the traditional tales became points of beginning and impetus to create something new. The humor, characterizations, the view of God as not consistently all-knowing are mine. Regarding God with a loving irreverence is characteristic of African American storytelling and is a tone I have applied in stories about God throughout my career. (See my *Black Folktales* for the earliest example.)

I also decided not to use a male image of God exclusively. In part this stemmed from my being accustomed to the Hebrew names for God and their connotations. In the Hebrew Bible, God is referred to by many names, each representing a different aspect of his being, that is, a different mode of expression. When one reads the Bible in Hebrew, one is aware of a difference in God's intent through the name used. The two names used in the first three chapters of Genesis are Elohim (Eh-low-heem) and Adonai (Ah-doe-nye), translated respectively as "God" and "Lord." Elohim represents God acting in his aspect of Justice. Adonai represents God acting in his aspect of Mercy.

Thus in English when the words "Lord God" are used, it is to indicate that God is acting with the qualities of Mercy and Justice. However, the word "Lord" has vastly different connotations for the Christian reader, and so I have refrained from using the word here.

Instead I use a variety of images for God—male, female, and imagistic: a bird, a mountain, rose petals, and other things. Some readers might be disturbed or even offended by this. Others will undoubtedly be confused. My intent is to invite the reader into a new experience of the Divine. One way to do this is to use new language. And who knows? Maybe God is tired of being thought of as an old man with a long white beard.

Let me add that the nontraditional images of God in these stories are not Jewish, and I do not put them forward as being so. They sprang from my imagination and reflect aspects of my experiences of and relationship with the Divine.

Hebrew reveals dimensions of experience and meaning unavailable in English translations. This is most evident, perhaps, in the story of the Fall, as it is called in Christian tradition. In Christianity, there is the doctrine of original sin stemming from Adam and Eve's eating the forbidden fruit. However, the concept of original sin does not exist in Judaism. For Jews, Adam and Eve's transgression is not their disobedience and eating of the fruit but their not accepting responsibility for the transgression. That interpretation of the story is traditional and would not be evident to someone who had not studied Torah in Hebrew as well as the primary rabbinic commentaries and midrashim.

Through the imagination sacred text can come alive in ways not possible otherwise. Through the imagination a sense of play is brought into our relationship to religion and God. In one of Isak Dinesen's short stories, a character says that God must be very lonely because no one ever plays with him.

That is what I have sought to do here—play with God. Play expresses the holy as surely as solemn piety. Maybe more so sometimes.

J. L.
Belchertown, Massachusetts
April 16, 1996–February 25, 1997

Pronunciation Guide

"Satan" and "Adam" are familiar English words. However, they are originally Hebrew. Because these are Jewish legends, the Jewish origin of these stories will be enhanced if Satan and Adam are pronounced as they are in Hebrew. This might also be of real assistance to the Christian reader who knows these figures in a Christian context but not their original Jewish one.

The letter *a* in Hebrew is always pronounced "ah."

The letter *e* is pronounced in one of two ways: "a" as in *able*, or "eh" as in *better*.

The letter *i* is pronounced as "ee" as in *easy*.

Adam is pronounced "Ah-dahm."

Adonai is pronounced "Ah-doe-nye."

Aviva is pronounced "Ah-vee-vah."

Chavah is the Hebrew name for "Eve." There is no English equivalent sound for the Hebrew *ch*, which is guttural. The *a*'s are pronounced as in "Sah-tahn" and "Ah-dahm."

Elohim is pronounced "Eh-low-heem."

Gabriel is pronounced "Gahb-ree-ehl."

Labbiel is pronounced "Lah-bee-ehl."

Lailah is pronounced "Lye-lah."

Lillith is pronounced "Lee-leet."

Meshabber is pronounced "Meh-shah-behr."

Raphael is pronounced "Reh-fah-ehl."

Re'em is pronounced "Reh-ehm."

Satan is pronounced "Sah-tahn."

Shabbat is pronounced "Shah-baht."

Shamir is pronounced "Shah-meer."

Tehom is pronounced "Teh-hom."

Yubal is pronounced "Yoo-bahl."

Zabua is pronounced "Zah-boo-ah."

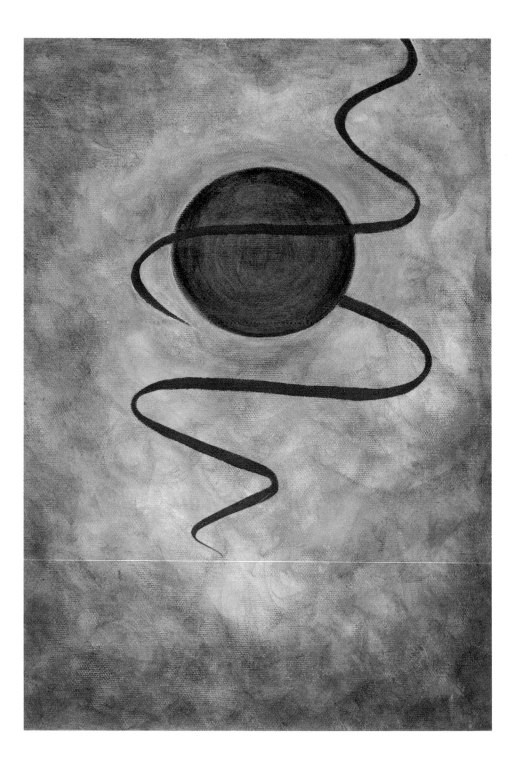

GENESIS 1:1–5: *When God began creating the heaven and the earth, the earth was empty and void and darkness was on the face of the abyss. And the spirit of God brooded on the face of the waters. And God said, Let there be light. And there was light. And God saw the light. It was good. And God separated the light from the darkness. And God called to the light, Day! and to the darkness God called, Night! And there was morning and there was evening. One day.*

....

CHAPTER ONE

God Learns How To Create

MAKING THE WORLD was not easy. If God hadn't been careful, there might be fish that bark, alligators walking into grocery stores and buying kosher hot dogs, and people sitting on nests and laying eggs. However, we do have mosquitoes, hay fever, cold sheets, brussels sprouts, and hiccups. Maybe God was not as careful as he could have been.

God would not have gotten into the creation business if he had had something to do. But there was just him and the angels—sitting in the dark. This darkness was unlike anything that ever was or will be. It had no top, bottom, or middle and was thick, like a question that could never be answered. Not only was it impossible to see through, you couldn't move against it. But since there was nowhere to go, that did not cause a problem.

All they did was sit. It was so dark they didn't even know they were sitting. Since they couldn't see anything or go anywhere, there was nothing to talk about—except how dark it was. Once a day or once every million years—what did they know?—Moe, Aviva, Jennifer, or one of the other angels would say, "Sure is dark."

"Sure is," God agreed.

Everybody would sigh and that was that. Another day or million years would pass and somebody else would say, "Sure is dark, God."

If God was feeling talkative he would reply, "You told the truth about that."

So it went for a tritillion years.

Then one day God blurted in anguish, "There has to be *something* to do."

"But what?" Sara asked, also in despair. She was the angel who sat on God's right, or thought she did. In reality, Sara wasn't near God at all. It only seemed that way because she understood him better than anyone else.

"I don't know," God said sadly.

Silence returned as heavy as yesterday's mistakes.

It lasted a long time before suddenly God said, "What was that?"

"What was what?" Aviva asked. She hadn't noticed anything.

"Something just went through my mind," God replied.

"An idea?" Sara wanted to know.

"No. A word."

"A word?" she repeated, getting excited.

"A *new* word," he said again. "But I don't know what it means."

"Sometimes things don't make sense until you say them out loud," Sara told him.

"Is that so?"

"Well, I think it is. What was the word?"

God hesitated. "It doesn't make any sense. If I say it aloud, I'll make a fool of myself. Nobody will know what I'm talking about, including me." God laughed, embarrassed.

"Maybe the word will let you know what it means."

God thought about that. "Well, all right." He sighed. "Light," he mumbled.

"Speak up, God," Sara encouraged him.

"*Light!*" he yelled.

No sooner was the word said than the darkness vanished. The

angels looked around. They could see each other! There they were, sitting on clouds like wishes on the razor blade of hope in a brightness going from evermore to evermore without stopping to catch its breath. They laughed with delight as they put faces to the voices they had been hearing since before forever. The angels had a grand time visiting with each other and especially examining their wings, which they had not known they had.

"So that's why I've had a backache since I can remember," Moe commented.

"You think you've had a backache, look at him!" Jennifer said, pointing to an angel with six wings growing from his shoulders.

"We only have two wings. Why does he have six?"

They didn't know and immediately looked for Sara. But when they found her, she didn't know, either.

"There's another one with six wings," Moe said. "Hey!"

The angel stopped and came over to them.

"Why do you have six wings and we only have two?" Moe asked.

The angel shrugged. "I've been wondering the same thing," he said.

Just then an angel flew toward them who had not two, not six, but *twelve* wings!

"Pardon me," Moe called politely.

The angel stopped.

"We noticed that you have twelve wings. Could you be—be, I mean, are you God?"

The angel laughed but it was a harsh sound that hurt the heart instead of gladdening it. "Not yet," he said. "I am called Satan."

"I am Michael," the angel with six wings introduced himself. "Do you know why we have more wings than some of the other angels?" he asked Satan.

Satan shook his head.

"Let's ask God," Jennifer said.

"Where is he?" Moe asked.

"I haven't seen him," Jennifer answered.

"How do you know? What does God look like?" Aviva put in.

Nobody knew. They looked and looked but there was nobody who looked like they thought God should look, that is, like them but bigger.

Then Sara noticed long ribbons of soft red light undulating above them in circles as wide as the future. She gazed at them with awe. Suddenly she knew. "God? Is that you?" she asked softly.

There was a long silence. Finally a voice as pure as unheard silence said, "For right now." God laughed as if beginning to understand who he was.

The angels gawked at the ribbons. This was not how they had thought God would look.

"Surprised?" God said, a smile in his voice.

"Uh, yes," Michael responded.

"I thought you looked like us," Moe put in.

"So did I," Jennifer agreed.

God was silent. He decided not to tell them. They would find out soon enough.

"God? Can I ask you a question?" Sara said hesitantly.

"Anything you want."

"Why does Michael have six wings and Satan twelve?"

"The angels with six wings like Michael, Gabriel, and Labbiel are leaders of clans. Satan has twelve wings because he is the Prince of Angels and my special assistant."

Satan grinned broadly.

Sara wanted to protest. She would be a better assistant than this, this Satan. She wanted to tell God so but didn't get the chance because suddenly he shouted, "There went another one!"

"Another what?" asked Aviva.

"Another word!"

Sara laughed in anticipation. "Let's hear it!"

"*World!*" God shouted.

A large ball of blue appeared in the distance. It was suspended in the light and turned slowly like love discovering itself.

4

The angels gazed at it in silent amazement and bewilderment.

"What's a world?" Jennifer asked finally.

"That's a good question," God responded. "That's a gooooood question!" Even he wasn't sure. But he didn't have time to think about it because words began rushing into his mind almost faster than he could say them.

"Purple rain!"

"Amber waves of grain!"

"Yellow submarine!"

"The internet!"

"Bagels, lox, and cream cheese!"

"Bugs!"

Major mistake. Heaven was suddenly filled with little tiny things whining and buzzing in the angels' ears, biting their arms, flying in their ears, up their noses, and under their robes.

"You could've stopped after the bagels, lox, and cream cheese," Moe told him between bites.

But God was having too much fun saying words and seeing what appeared. He didn't know what to do with all the things so angels scurried to put them in closets until he figured it out. Before long, there were closets all over heaven. Some were stuffed with trees, clouds, birds, whales, lions, elephants, and such. Others were crammed with things God knew he wouldn't use, like red grass, fish with mustaches, rain that fell up, candy-striped gorillas, white darkness, and constant sorrow.

Finally God ran out of words, and not a minute too soon. There was no place to put another closet.

"Now what?" Sara asked.

"I'm done for today," God answered. "Get some sleep. The next few days are going to be busy."

And God said, Bind the waters under the heavens in one place and let dry land be seen. And it was so. And God called to the dry land, Earth! and to the binding of the waters he called Seas! And God saw. It was good.

. . . .

CHAPTER TWO

God Battles the Queen of the Waters

THE ANGELS WERE UP early the next morning, eager to see what God was going to do next. But God wasn't there. At least, he wasn't there looking like ribbons.

"Where's God?" Michael asked Sara.

Sara shook her head, then smiled. "He's here somewhere. I think God likes to play." She looked around until she noticed a dark green light. "There!" she exclaimed. "I've never seen a light that color."

As if in answer, the light flashed like the instant a heart beats for the first time.

"Hi, God!" Sara shouted.

"Hi, Sara!" the voice said from the light. "You are good at finding me."

Sara smiled. "It's not hard. So, what's next?"

"I'm going to start decorating the world. But first I have to do something about the water. There's too much of it."

"Water?" Moe asked.

"The blue covering the world. That's water."

"What're you going to do?"

"Watch," said the voice from within the throbbing light. "Let the waters be gathered together!" it called out.

The waters started to pull back and the brown earth beneath began to show.

"*No!*" came a voice that no one, not even God, had ever heard.

The waters stopped.

Then they reversed direction and moved forward, threatening to cover the earth once more.

"Who said that?" God wanted to know. "What's going on? Why are the waters disobeying me?"

As if in answer, the waters rose up like anger and curled into large waves as if sneering at God. Then, he saw. At the top of the highest wave, straddling it like a horse, sat a woman. Her hair was long and yellow and streamed down her back like combed strands of light. Her skin was a blue as warm as a baby's smile. She spread her arms and the waters stopped, suspended like Time holding its breath.

"Who—who are you?" God asked.

"I am Tehom, Queen of the Waters. Who are you?"

"I am God. I—I made all this," he answered.

"God. What an odd name. Couldn't your parents have picked something better?"

"I am my parent," God answered, indignant, "and yours, too—I think."

"Sure you are," Tehom rejoined sarcastically. "What do you think you're doing to my waters?"

"There're too many of them. They need to make room for dry land and all I am going to put on it."

Tehom laughed derisively. "Go make another world. This one is mine."

"We'll see about that," God replied.

Suddenly the light exploded and God turned into a woman with skin as brilliantly black as the backside of lightning and hair as green as a flower's heart. She snapped her fingers and a horse of fire appeared. God leaped onto its back, grabbed the horse's mane, and galloped out of heaven.

Down, down, down, God came, flinging hail, wind, and lightning at Tehom. So furiously did God throw the forces of nature at Tehom that the waves began shrinking back in terror. Tehom toppled from her perch and tumbled into the waters.

"Let the waters be gathered together!" God shouted.

Once again the waters began to recede, revealing the brown earth beneath. The waters continued going down until the mountains and hills were revealed. Finally, the waters stopped and they became the seas.

"So this is what a world looks like," God said to herself, pleased by what she saw.

Just then Tehom burst from the sea, but her face twisted with rage. "Noooooo! How dare you take my world from me!" she shouted. "I will not allow it! Who do you think you are?"

The horse of fire reared on its hind legs, and God shouted in a voice that is still resounding through infinity, "I am God, Creator of All!"

"We shall see about that," Tehom laughed. "Reclaim the world!" she shouted to the waters.

In response to their queen's voice, the waters began rising again. God sprang from the horse and onto Tehom. Grabbing her long hair, God pulled her down into the waters. Tehom struggled, trying to loosen God's grasp, but God scarcely noticed. Down, down, down, she pulled the Queen of the Waters.

Rapidly God swam over the mountains that rise up from the ocean floor until she reached a canyon. Holding Tehom's hair with a grip like teeth, God dove to the deepest part of the canyon until she came to a gate in the ocean floor.

"Where did this come from?" Tehom asked, thrashing futilely to free herself from God's grasp.

Even God was unsure.

When she had heard Tehom's Noooooo! explode from the waters, a picture of this place had come into her mind. And here it was!

God opened the gate, thrust Tehom inside, and locked it. Tehom screamed and yelled and shook the gate, but God had already shot up from the ocean floor and onto the land where the waters were continuing to rise.

Quickly God walked around the world, encircling the waters. Everywhere she stepped, the dirt beneath her feet crumbled into tiny pieces, and that's how sand came into being.

The waters were furious at God for imprisoning their queen and furious that God dared try to confine them. Did God think mere bits of dirt could stop them from ruling the world? Raising themselves as high as a selfish thought, the waters fell down toward the sand.

The grains of sand screamed as they saw the giant waves coming at them.

"You are very tiny," God said quickly to the sand, "but if you stay close to each other, not even the mighty waters can hurt you."

The grains of sand moved tightly together and closed their tiny eyes as the waters fell on them with a great roar. The waves had thought they could stand atop the sand like they had the mountains. But when they reached for something to climb up they started slipping. They scrambled and clawed and scratched trying to get a footing but slid back into the valleys where God intended them to be. Again and again they rose up and slammed onto the sand, and each time they slipped and slid back into the valleys.

To this day, the waters are angry. From beneath the floor of the deepest canyon at the bottom of the sea, Tehom calls constantly, telling them to rise up and reclaim the world. All day and all night the waters try, but the sands are there to hold them back.

GENESIS 1:14–18: *And God said, Let there be lights in the foundation of the heaven to separate between the day and between the night and they will be for signs and for seasons and for days and for years. And they will be for lights in the foundation of the heaven to light the earth. And it was so. And God made two big lights and the bigger light ruled the day and the smaller light ruled the night and the stars. And God put them in the foundation of heaven to light the earth and rule over the day and night and separate between the light and between the darkness and God saw. It was good.*

••

CHAPTER THREE

Sun and Moon

THE ANGELS HAD WITNESSED the battle down on the world and were confused.

"What was that all about?" Aviva asked.

"And who was that who came out of the water?" Gabriel wanted to know.

"I'm not sure," Michael answered.

"And who was that with skin like darkness riding the horse of fire?" Aviva asked.

"I think that was God," Jennifer put in.

Moe shook his head. "Couldn't have been. God looks like ribbons of light."

"What if," Sara began, wonder filling her voice, "what if God can look like anything or anyone? What if God can change whenever he wants and be whatever he wants?"

"Are you serious?" Satan returned, shocked.

"I am."

"Do you mean God can be a he, a she, or an it?" Gabriel asked.

"I think so," Sara told him.

"Do you realize what this means?" Satan asked.

"It means we can never be sure when we're seeing God," answered Alexander.

"That's right!" Satan agreed. "We can't ever be sure when we're talking to God and when we aren't."

"I'm not sure I like that," Jennifer offered. "I want to know who I'm talking to and I *really* want to know when I'm talking to God."

They were silent for a moment. Finally, Sara said softly, "Maybe it just means we should talk to everyone as if it was God."

"It was easier when God was just a voice in the darkness," Moe offered, rejecting Sara's idea as if it were the most ridiculous thing he had ever heard. "I knew who God was then. I don't feel like he's one of us anymore."

"That's true," Michael added, unhappy. "God doesn't care about anything now except that world of his and what he can do to it."

Still in the form of a woman dark as love and riding the horse of fire, God heard the angels talking as she came closer to heaven. She turned into a golden band and encircled the heavens like a wedding song.

"Look!" Satan exclaimed. "Is—is that who I think it is?"

Jennifer smiled. "God has returned."

The angels were silent as if hypnotized by the shining band holding them in its glow. Although they were still afraid of all the forms God might assume, something in them was also a little curious as to how God might appear next.

God was eager to get back to work but he needed more light. He changed into a yellow bird with wings as wide as dawn. Taking some of the light, God shaped it into a ball of fire bigger than the world and set it in the foundation of heaven. That was the Sun. Then he took more light and shaped it into a white ball the same size. That was the Moon.

Suddenly the angels felt warm.

"What's going on?" Michael wanted to know.

"Feels good," Jennifer put in.

"Speak for yourself," Moe responded. "God is making too many

changes. What was wrong with the darkness? Weren't you happier when it was dark?"

"I hated it," Satan said.

Moe shook his head. "We don't need those two big lights up there. We don't need this warmth."

"But it sure is nice," said Aviva.

The Sun was pleased at these words. He was so happy to be alive. Every morning from that first one until this one, Sun started singing the minute he woke up. "I am the Sun. Yes, yes, yes! I will make you warm. Yes, yes, yes. I will give you light. Yes, yes, yes. I am the Suuuuuunnnn!"

(It wouldn't have been so bad if he had been able to carry a tune.)

Sun didn't care. He enjoyed being Sun so much that the heat from his joy would have burned up the world if he had not taken a shower every morning and cooled it off. After breakfast Sun put on his red, yellow, and orange suit and strutted out of the house, a big grin on his face, and got in his chariot. Ninety-six angels were lined up behind the chariot and they went with Sun on his journey, eight every hour—two to the left, two to the right, two in front, and two behind. Following them were the Chalkadri. They were nine hundred miles big, with crocodile heads, lion tails, and twelve wings, and were the same shade of purple as in the rainbow. They walked beside Sun's chariot next to the angels. The chariot was pulled by two winds, one shaped like a bird with the body of a snake and the other like a snake with the face of a lion. When everyone was in place, Sun rode off, grinning as if listening to never-ending applause.

Before he went home every evening, Sun would stop by God's house to tell him what he had seen on earth that day. When he finished his report, God would tell him, "You're a wonderful Sun. Thank you for being you." Sun was so pleased by God's praise that he blushed purple and orange. The colors would spread across the sky, and that's why there are sunsets. Whenever you see one, God has just told Sun what a good job he did that day.

Around the time Sun was blushing, Moon would wake up. Sun and Moon lived next door to each other, and Moon heard him as he came home from work every evening, singing, of course. "I am the Sun. I have brought you warmth. I have brought you light. I'll be back tomorrow to do it again!! I am, I am, I am the Suuuuuunnnn!!!"

Moon would sigh and put on her white robe. Why was Sun always so happy? she wondered. What was there to be happy about *all* the time? "He isn't really that happy. He's just showing off," she murmured. "God didn't make him better than me. God made us equal. You don't see me going around singing about how wonderful I am—even though I am."

Moon became more and more irritated listening to Sun sing his own praises day after day. Finally, one morning as she finished work and stepped out of the sky, she said, "I'm going to put a stop to his noise."

On her way home she stopped by God's house and knocked on the door.

"Be there in a minute," came the voice from within.

Just as you decide what clothes to put on every morning, God has to decide who or what to look like each day. He would walk around the house as a lion or giraffe, hop like a grasshopper or rabbit, float like a butterfly or dandelion pod. What he liked most, though, were shapes, and he had learned to make himself into a rhombus of rain, a circle of cicadas, a square of squirrels, and a triangle of troglodytes.

God had not decided yet who or what he wanted to look like that day, so he became the ribbons of light. "Come in," he called.

"Good morning, God," Moon greeted the ribbons as she came inside.

"Good morning to you, Moon. Come on in. So, tell me. What do you think of my world?"

"Oh, I think it is wonderful, God. And I'm glad you brought it up because that's what I came to talk to you about."

"You've got my full attention."

Moon smiled, pleased. "As I go through the sky I have time to observe the world and to think. From my observations it seems you made heaven greater than earth."

"That's right."

"You made water stronger than fire because water can put out fire."

"That's right."

"And you made air stronger than dirt because air can blow dirt away."

"That's right."

"Well, since all of that is true, there's something I don't understand."

"You've got my curiosity wide awake, Moon. Where could I have gone wrong?"

"Why did you make me and Sun equal? Shouldn't one of us be greater and stronger than the other?"

God sighed. He had thought she was going to teach him something about his world that he didn't know. All she wanted was to be superior to Sun.

God was silent for a long time and Moon began to feel uncomfortable. Had she said something wrong? All she had done was ask a question.

Finally God spoke. "I am disappointed in you," he said, his voice sad. "You want to be greater than Sun. You envy his joy instead of finding your own. If you were filled with gratitude for what I gave you, you would scarcely notice Sun. Because you are ungrateful, I am going to make you the smaller one and take away all but a little of your light. From now on your light will change continually. Sometimes your face will be full; other times only a sliver will show. Sometimes you will not be seen at all."

Moon gasped. "But, but, God!" she exclaimed, and started to cry. "That is such a harsh punishment. Is gratitude that important?" she asked in a small voice.

"Without gratitude, there is nothing," God answered firmly.

Moon left God's house with tears flowing from her eyes and into the air. When Moon got home her crying was so loud, Sun heard her in his house. He was so upset he didn't sing in the shower that morning and before he rode off in his chariot, he went next door to find out what was hurting her, but she did not answer his knock.

Moon was small now and her light faint. For many nights Moon cried as she moved across the sky. The tears flowed constantly from her eyes and streamed into the air where they began to glow with the heat of remorse and shame.

To this day Moon's tears can be seen in the sky. They are the stars.

GENESIS 1:11–12, 20–21, 24–25: *And God said, Let the earth sprout vegetation, herbs with their seeds, fruit trees and their seeds, making fruit after their kind on the earth, and it was so. And the earth brought forth vegetation and herbs with their seeds and fruit trees and their seeds, making fruit after their kind on the earth. And God saw. It was good.*

And God said, Let the waters move with moving souls and let flying creatures fly about the earth and in front of the foundation of heaven. And God created the great sea giants and every living soul that creeps and crawls with which the waters moved after their kind and every winged flying creature after their kind. And God saw. It was good.

And God said, Let the earth bring forth living souls after its kind, cattle and creeping things and beasts of the earth after its kind. And God made the beasts of the earth after their kind and the cattle after their kind and all that creeps on the ground after their kind. And God saw. It was good.

* *

CHAPTER FOUR

Strange Creatures

NOW THAT GOD HAD all the light he needed, it was time to get back to work. He changed into a broad flame of soft blue and orange and swept over the earth. Grasses, bushes, flowers, trees, herbs, vegetables, and everything that grows sprouted into being as the flame passed.

"Look!" Sara called.

The angels stared down at the world. Where before it had been only browns and blues, now there were also greens.

"Isn't it beautiful?" Aviva asked.

"It is," Satan agreed. "But why doesn't God make it that beautiful up here?"

"What's he doing now?" Moe interrupted.

God changed into a tornado-shaped funnel of reds and oranges and spun across the world again. Out of the funnel scampered animals—cows, horses, sheep, dogs, cats, elephants, tigers, dinosaurs, lions, monkeys, and birds—running, galloping, leaping, flying.

"I wish I could go down there!" Alexander exclaimed.

God changed into the circle as golden as a wedding band and grew wider and wider until he surrounded the world. He had intended to relax for a few minutes and enjoy looking at his beautiful world, but suddenly there came a roar so loud it seemed to bounce off the four corners of the universe.

"What was that?" God looked around anxiously, afraid Tehom had escaped from the prison at the bottom of the sea, but he didn't see her. The roar came again and almost knocked Sun out of his chariot. This time God saw who was making the noise. It was Lion!

Back then Lion was bigger than he is now. His head reached the top of the tallest tree and the hair from his mane flowed down to the ground in a long silken stream. Lion walked around like he was the Sun on four feet. Like Sun, Lion was happy that he was who he was and had to let everybody know. That was the roar God had heard.

Every time Lion thought about how good it was to be lion, well, he had to roar. *Roaaarrrrrr!* That particular roar of happiness knocked down all the trees for four hundred miles in every direction. Lion strutted on his way, feeling even better.

He walked a hundred miles and got to thinking again about how wonderful it was to be lion and—*Roaaarrrrrr!* Mountains crumbled five hundred miles away.

"I can't have something in the world that loud!" God exclaimed. "If that lion gets any happier, I won't have any world left."

God took Lion and tied his mouth with rope made of twined fire. Who knows? That lion is probably still running around somewhere looking for someone to untie his jaw so he can give one last roar.

God liked Lion so he made a new one, but smaller. That's the one in the world today. He is still King of the Beasts and looks just like that first lion and his roar is the same, too. But it's a lot quieter.

When God made some of the creatures he got a little too creative. That's what happens when you can do anything you want. Just because you *can* make something, it doesn't mean you *should.* God did not know that yet.

The Re'em are two of the ugliest creatures to ever walk the earth. However, they might also be the two most beautiful. We'll never know for sure because the only person to ever see them was King David and he was so scared he didn't pay any attention to their looks.

When he was a boy, he was out tending his father's sheep one day and herded them up a steep mountain, one he'd never noticed. Up and up and up the sheep went and David right behind them. When they got close to the top, something strange happened. The mountain stood up. Up and up and up the mountain rose until David and the sheep were looking over the ceiling of the sky and into heaven on the other side.

David didn't know it, but he and the sheep had walked up the horn of a Re'em. God saw what the problem was and told the Re'em to lie back down. Slowly, the Re'em lowered itself and David and the sheep scampered down the horn and back to earth where they belonged.

God only made two Re'em and they didn't live together. The female resided in the east. The male stayed in the west. For seventy years they didn't do anything except lie around and sleep and eat. But in the seventieth year the female began singing a high-pitched song that only the male could hear, even though he was at the other end of the earth. He answered with a low-pitched song only she could hear. Singing, they made their way toward each other and eventually met where east and west come together, and there, the Re'em made a baby.

If the male Re'em had known better, he might have had second thoughts because as soon as the female knew she was pregnant, she bit him on the neck and he fell over and died. Then again, if the female had had any sense, she would've stayed home because she was pregnant for eleven years. When the twelfth year started, she was so heavy that she slumped to the ground. (She was also very tired of standing up.) She lay there, unable to move. The saliva from her mouth watered the ground around her. This made the grasses grow, so she had food to eat.

At the end of the year, she gave birth to two children and then she died. One child was male and he went to the east. The other was female and she went to the west. Seventy years later it started all over again. Only God and the angels know if the Re'em are still around and where they are.

As God was making the world and everything in it, on it, and above it, he realized that sometimes he might need some assistants to help him keep an eye on it all. Thus he made Ziz, Behemoth, and Leviathan.

Ziz was in charge of the birds. Back in ancient times Ziz lived among people, and once some people on a ship saw Ziz standing in the water, its head touching the foundation of the heaven. Noticing that they could see Ziz's ankles, the people thought the water was not very deep. They told the ship's captain to stop. It was a hot day and a swim would be nice. Just as the people were about to get in the water, however, God called out in a great voice, "Stop! Seven years ago someone dropped his ax in the water at just this place and it has still not reached the bottom."

Once Ziz tried to put an egg in its nest but missed. The egg fell to the earth and burst. The sound alone crushed a forest of giant trees and the fluid from the egg flooded sixty cities.

Ziz is so huge that when it spreads its wings, the sun is blotted out. Sometimes when you think a cloud has passed in front of the sun, it might be the shadow of Ziz's wings. Ziz's wings have to be big because they protect the earth from the winds. If not for them, everything on earth would be blown away by the angry winds that are continually tearing dust from the ground and trying to uproot trees, houses, and people.

Every year on the day of the autumnal equinox, Ziz flaps its great wings and gives a loud cry. The wind from its wings rushes through the world and ruffles the feathers of all the birds, and the sound of its cry trembles their beaks and makes them afraid. This causes the hawks, eagles, and all the great birds of prey to remember that there is a bird more fierce than they. If not for this, they would eat every little creature they could.

Behemoth rules the creatures on land. When it lies down, it stretches across a thousand mountains, and every day eats all the vegetation on each and every mountain. Fortunately, the vegetation grows back at night. Behemoth is so thirsty God created a river especially for it. The river is called Yubal and it flows directly from the Garden of Eden to Behemoth's mouth.

Every year at the time of the summer solstice, Behemoth raises its head and roars once. The roar goes around the world but is heard only by the beasts and fierce animals. It reminds them that there is a creature more fierce than they. Afraid of what Behemoth might do to them, reluctantly they decide they will not eat the tame animals for another year.

Leviathan rules everything that lives in the seas. His eyes are so beautiful they radiate light through the oceans and give the fish their incredible colors. Whenever Leviathan lets out a breath that warms the waters, the other fish know he is hungry. The fish consider it a great honor to be Leviathan's food, so when the waters grow warm, they swim rapidly to Leviathan so he can have a choice of the tastiest fish to eat.

Every year at the winter solstice Leviathan sneezes. The waters churn and boil furiously and the big fish are reminded there is a creature in the waters more fierce than they. Afraid of what Leviathan might do to them, they decide not to eat all the little fish for another year.

Of all the creatures, Leviathan has the most special relationship with God. You see, God works twelve hours every day. The first three are devoted to studying Torah. During the next three he judges the world. Then he spends three hours feeding everything from the elephant to the gnat. Finally, God gets to relax for three hours. How does he do that? He plays with Leviathan, which is why Leviathan is known as God's playmate.

CHAPTER FIVE

The Angel of Death

SATISFIED WITH HOW well the work was going, it was time to talk with the angels. God knew they thought he had forgotten them. That wasn't true. Quite the contrary.

"Satan?" he said to his chief assistant. "Call the angels together for me."

"Why?" Satan asked sharply, wondering what God was up to.

God didn't like his tone of voice. "Because I said so," he responded emphatically.

"Yes, sir." Satan gulped. He sent his assistants—the angels with six wings—throughout heaven and they spread the word that God wanted to talk to them.

The angels gathered at heaven's center, which was at the junction of forever and a day. They were surprised by how many of them there were. In fact, a number big enough to count all the angels has never been invented. Even God was impressed at seeing them all together.

"Good morning, angels," he began.

"Good morning, God," they responded in unison. The sound of that many voices is still wandering through the universe looking for ears.

"Many of you think I have forgotten you, that I am more concerned about the world I am making. That is not so. I would never

25

forget about you. You have been with me always. You will be with me always."

A deep sigh of relief went out from the angels.

"Now that the world is almost finished," God continued, "it is time to tell you what I want you to do."

"Us?" they exclaimed to each other, incredulous.

"We're going to have a role in God's world?"

"Awesome!"

"What do you want us to do, God?" a quazillion angels asked.

"I want you to be guardians of everything and everyone in the world."

Silence. The angels stared at God blankly, as if waiting for him to go on.

God was puzzled by their lack of response. "I thought you would be excited," he said finally.

"Oh, we are," Aviva offered, to be polite.

It took Moe to ask the question that was on all their minds. "God? What's a guardian?"

God smiled, embarrassed. "Oh. Forgive me. A guardian watches over and cares for something. For example, the ninety-six angels who run beside Sun's chariot are his guardians. Everything in the world will need looking over, especially the people."

"What are people?" Sara asked immediately.

God cleared his throat, realizing that he had spoken too quickly. "Don't worry about it. You'll like them. I know you will."

"So, who gets to watch over what?" Michael wanted to know.

For the rest of the morning the angels went before God and received their assignments. He made Sara Angel of Mercy, Jennifer Angel of Clouds, Moe the Angel of Bagels, and Aviva Angel of Bugs. (She was weird, anyway.) There were so many angels that God was able to assign an angel to every blade of grass and every leaf on every tree. There were angels assigned to people who would not be born until the year 4711. There were angels whose job was to collect all the tears that would be shed, and angels

to gather all the smiles. There were angels who made people's dreams, once there were people, and others whose job was to make the really weird dreams, while still others specialized in nightmares. There was an Angel of Peculiar Odors, an Angel of Itching and Scratching, and, most absurd of all, an Angel of Absurdity.

There were so many angels, however, that even after all the jobs had been given out, there were many angels who didn't have jobs, and they felt left out.

"Don't worry," God reassured them. "The world is going to create things I have not thought of, and those things will need guardian angels. So, if you do not have a job now, don't worry. You will. However, there is one last job I need an angel for now and am not sure who that should be. The job is death."

The very sound of the word made the angels draw back. Angel of Death was not as nice a name as Angel of Orange Juice, or Angel of Softness. Everyone was as silent as—well—death.

Finally, a voice asked what they had all been wondering. "God? What's death?"

"Who asked that?" God asked.

A hand went up shyly. It belonged to a disheveled-looking angel whose wings were a bit lopsided and whose feet seemed to want to go in two directions at once.

"Who are you?" Satan asked.

"Meshabber," came the response.

"And why do you want to know what death is?" God asked.

Meshabber shrugged. "I don't know. Just curious, I guess."

God smiled to himself. "You remember what it was like when we sat in the dark all the time?"

"It was, well, like nothing," Meshabber responded. "Nothing to see. Nothing to do. We just sat there."

"That's what death is like—except you don't know it."

Meshabber scratched his head. "I kind of understand, but not really. Uh, what exactly would the Angel of Death do?"

"Everything that lives will one day die. It will be the Angel of Death's job to help them."

Meshabber thought for a minute. "Sure. Why not? I think I could do that. What do I do?"

"Go down to the world. Take two of every animal and throw them into the water. They will die and that is how the other animals will learn of death."

Meshabber flew to earth and went to work. Angels are very, very strong, even the smallest ones, and Meshabber was not big. But he picked up a pair of elephants by their ears, swung them around his head and flung them into the water. Tigers, buffalo, hippos, and all the other large animals followed quickly.

The animals who yet lived stood on the banks of the waters. They roared and snarled and snapped and made all kinds of animal noises as tears poured from their eyes.

"What's the matter?" Meshabber asked a rhinoceros.

"The animals you threw in the waters have not come back. They have sunk to the bottom and will never come back."

"Never?" Meshabber was shocked. "You mean, that's what death is?"

The rhino nodded. "I guess so."

Meshabber shook his head. He wasn't sure he was going to like this job after all. However, he had no choice. God expected him to do what he had said he would do. So, he started on the small animals—gophers, beavers, wolves, rabbits, and moles.

Meshabber grabbed a cat and started to throw it in the water when the cat screamed, "Hey! Stop! What do you think you're doing? Stooooop!!!"

Meshabber did just that. "What's the matter?" he wanted to know.

"Death is so awful," wept Cat. "One minute you have a friend and the next minute, you don't."

Cat pointed to the face of a cat in the water. She was pointing to her reflection but Meshabber didn't know that. (Among the angels, he was not known as a rocket scientist.) "That's your friend?" he asked Cat.

"One of them," Cat said, still weeping. "The other one sank down to the bottom."

Meshabber couldn't remember throwing two cats in the water, but all animals looked alike to him. "Well, lucky for you. If I hadn't already thrown those two cats in, I would have thrown you." He put Cat back on the ground.

Cat ran away as quickly as she could. And that's why to this day cats have nine lives. The first one tricked the Angel of Death.

Meshabber didn't know that he wasn't a very good Angel of Death. He wasn't very bright and could be fooled easily or talked into letting someone live a little longer.

And that was just the kind of Angel of Death God wanted.

CHAPTER SIX

Cat and Mouse

GOD'S PLAN WAS that everything in creation would get along with everything else. But just because he planned something didn't mean that was how it would be.

God intended for Cat and Mouse to be best friends. And they were—at first. But sometimes one person has more friend-feeling in his heart than the other person. That's how it was with Cat and Mouse.

One day Mouse saw God and said, "I've got a problem."

"Well, tell me about it."

"You made me and Cat to be best friends," Mouse began.

"That's true."

"It's not working out like that."

"What's the matter?"

"Cat is big and I am small and he eats a lot."

"So? Do you get enough to eat?"

Mouse nodded slowly. "Well, yes, but . . ."

"But what?" God asked.

"It's not fair that Cat eats so much."

"Why do you care?"

"It's—it's not that I care," Mouse stammered. "I just don't think it's fair."

God sighed. He had thought that all the things he created would be so happy and so grateful they were who they were that they wouldn't care about anything or anybody else. But that wasn't how it was working out. First Moon was jealous of Sun. Now Mouse was jealous of Cat.

God was silent for so long that Mouse began getting nervous. "Everything all right, God? I didn't say something wrong, did I?"

"I'm afraid you did," God responded.

"What? What did I say?" Mouse asked, very nervous and very scared now.

"You are not grateful for who you are. You cared more about what Cat put in his stomach than that your stomach was as big as it needed to be. Because you were ungrateful, from this day forward one of the things cats will be allowed to put in their stomach is mice."

"You're joking, right?" Mouse laughed nervously. "Cat would never eat me. We're as close as the wet in water."

God didn't say anything.

Warily, Mouse went home. "Naw, Cat would never eat me. We're good buddies," Mouse said to himself. But as he got closer to home, he noticed Cat a few feet behind him. Mouse glanced nervously over his shoulder. Cat wasn't walking. He was slinking. Mouse went faster. Cat went faster. Mouse glanced nervously over his shoulder again. Cat wasn't slinking. He was stalking.

Very quickly Mouse decided that if Cat was going to eat him, he had no choice but to eat Cat first. Mouse stopped suddenly, spun around, and ran at Cat and bit him on the leg.

Cat blinked dumbly, as he barely felt Mouse's bite. Then, as silent as a tear, Cat leaped on Mouse and ate him.

And, from that day to this, cats eat mice.

God was sad. This was not how he had wanted the world to be. But to be ungrateful? That was something God would never understand.

CHAPTER SEVEN

Leviathan and Fox

GOD WAS SAD about Mouse. He decided to cheer himself and go play with Leviathan for a little while. God dove into the water and became a large dolphin, but Leviathan wasn't in a playful mood that day. He wanted to talk.

God sighed. He hoped Leviathan wasn't going to complain about something.

"God? If I am not mistaken, you made me the smartest creature in the water."

"That's true."

"Who did you make the smartest on land?"

"If I tell you, are you going to ask me to make that creature less intelligent?"

"Not at all," Leviathan reassured God.

"Well, I'm not sure who's the smartest. It is either Cat or Fox, but Owl is no dummy, either."

Leviathan shook his head. "It's not Cat. He's just smarter than Death and Death is not smart at all. I don't want it to be Owl."

"Why not?" God asked.

Leviathan shrugged. "Limited vocabulary. All he says is, 'Who? Who? Who?' Who cares? That's what I say. So, the smartest animal

on land has got to be Fox. And that leads to my next question, God. Who's smarter? Me or Fox?"

"The question never occurred to me. What does it matter?"

Leviathan shrugged. "I don't know. It just does."

God sighed. "I'll come back later when you feel like playing." He leaped from the water and turned into a large yellow bird and floated on the upper currents of wind, curious to see what Leviathan was going to do.

"Bring Fox to me!" Leviathan called out.

A squad of powerful fish swam until they came to the river and cruised close to the shore looking for Fox. It was a while before they saw him come strolling up the riverbank.

Fox saw the fish and began drooling. "I wish I could eat fish like these all the time."

The fish swam close to Fox, their bodies glistening silver sleek. "Follow us! We will take you where you can eat as many fish as you want for the rest of your life," the leader said.

"For real?" Fox responded, excited.

"Not only that, you're going to receive a great honor."

"Me?"

"You!"

"What? What?" Fox was so excited the red on his tail almost came off.

"Leviathan, the ruler of all the creatures of the sea, is about to die. The next ruler is supposed to be the smartest creature on land, and that is you. Leviathan wants to meet you before he dies."

"Can I have fish for dinner?" Fox wanted to know.

"As much as you can eat," the leader reassured him.

Fox didn't need to hear another word. "How do I get to this Leviatongue?"

"We will carry you on our backs to his throne."

Fox's tail twitched as he looked at the currents of the river rippling like anger. Then he stared warily at the fish and put a paw out tentatively toward their shiny, slippery, silvery backs.

"Don't worry," the leader reassured him. "Just think. You'll soon be eating all the fish you want."

Fox stepped gingerly onto their backs, a leg on each one. With a quick flick of their fins, off they went. The farther from shore they swam, the more nervous Fox became. What did a fox know about water? And, why would the King of the Fish want to make him the new king? The more Fox thought about it, the more two plus two did not make four.

"Fish?" Fox called nervously.

"What's on your mind?" the leader asked.

"Why would Leviatennis want to make a fox King of the Fish?"

Fox was as smart as Leviathan said he was, the fish thought. "You're right. Leviathan will not die until the end of the world comes, and that's a long time off yet."

"So, what's going on?"

The leader thought there was no danger in telling Fox because they were far enough from land that Fox couldn't get away. "Leviathan wants your heart."

"He wants my *what*?"

"He wants to be as smart as you are, and wisdom lies in the heart."

Fox snorted. "I wish you had told me," he said indignantly. "If you had, I would have brought my heart with me."

"I beg your pardon?" the leader said, slowing down.

"I said I would have brought my heart with me."

"You don't have your heart with you?"

"Are you kidding? Foxes don't go around with their hearts. If we did, the other creatures would always be trying to get our wisdom and we wouldn't have time to get anything done." Fox started laughing. "Boy, is Leviaturkey going to be mad if you guys bring me to him without my heart!"

The fish stopped. "Where is your heart?"

Fox shook his head. "Can't tell you. We foxes keep our hearts in a secret place."

"We'll take you back and you can go to your secret place and get your heart."

"Sure," Fox agreed. "No problemo."

The fish turned around and sped back to where they had found Fox. Even before they came to a stop at the shore, Fox had jumped off their backs and onto the riverbank. "Thank you very much!" he called to the fish, laughing.

"What are you doing?" the leader asked. "Go get your heart so we can take you to Leviathan."

Fox looked at them. "Are you as dumb as you act? Do you think I could talk to you if I didn't have my heart inside my body going bumpity-bump? Bumpity-bump. Is there a creature anywhere that can go around without a heart? I don't think so."

"You're joking," the fish said.

Fox laughed. "Don't worry about it. Go tell Leviashorts he is smart but not as smart as I am."

When the fish told Leviathan what Fox said, Leviathan nodded his head. "Fox is very smart indeed."

And high in the sky above the river, a yellow bird sang a song of laughter.

CHAPTER EIGHT

Crow Learns a Lesson

GOD WAS VERY SAD that some of his creations were not satisfied with how he had made them. They thought they knew better than he did who they should be or what they should look like.

God decided he would have a talk with the creatures to see if they were all unhappy. Because he wanted them to be honest with him, he thought a long time about what shape to assume. It had to be one that would make them feel they could say what was on their minds. Finally, it came to him.

God changed into a flower.

The first creature that came was Giraffe. "What were you thinking about when you made me?" Giraffe began, without even a good morning, God. "Am I or am I not the most ridiculous thing on the earth? My neck is longer than my legs. I have to sleep standing up. True, I can see long distances but what does it matter since there is nothing to see."

Next was Crab. She complained that she couldn't walk in a straight line, only sideways. Whale said he couldn't stand being wet all the time. Dog was upset because he had a lot he wanted to say but the only word God gave him was "Arf! Arf!" Mole said he was claustrophobic and being in the ground was driving him nuts, while the birds said it was exhausting having to move their wings constantly to keep from falling out of the sky.

On and on and on it went, creature after creature after creature. No one was pleased with who they were. God listened and got more and more depressed. Finally, when the last creature had spoken its piece, God sighed.

"I thought I knew what I was doing. Maybe I didn't. If you don't like how I made you and can figure out a way to change it, you can do that."

A great cheer went up and chaos was created as Whale, who really wanted to be a bird, leaped from the waters and tried to perch himself at the top of a tree. After a while, though, he had trouble breathing and hurried back into the water. Mole, who secretly longed to be a fish, jumped in the water and promptly sank to the bottom. He would have drowned if Leviathan hadn't tossed him back onto the land. And so it went as the creatures tried to be somebody else and learned they could only be who they were. Except for Crow.

God had made Crow with powerful wings and legs, which enabled him to walk as well as he could fly. That was fine except Crow wanted to be a dove. Nothing in creation was as graceful as a dove, thought Crow. "If I could walk like that, I would be the happiest bird alive," Crow said.

Every day Crow hid himself in a tree and watched the doves walk by. He loved the way their heads bobbed and the short, soft steps of their walk. The more he observed them, the more ashamed he was of his big body and long steps and stiff neck. He was sure the doves laughed at him and probably all the other birds did, too.

Crow was so ashamed of his walk that he decided not to leave his house until he could walk like a dove. So he practiced. One week, two weeks, and finally, near the end of the third week, Crow was satisfied. His walk was now so much like a dove's that all the

other birds would think he was one, even if his feathers were still as black as wisdom.

The next morning he came out of his house and, sure enough, the other birds were amazed to see him walk. They would've thought he was a dove except he looked like a crow.

"Hey, Crow. Why are you walking like a dove? You're a crow," Robin called.

"Hey, Crow. You're walking like you have a cramp in your craw," Buzzard shouted.

"You walk like you need to go to the bathroom real bad," Turkey said.

Crow ignored them. In his mind he was walking the prettiest walk that had ever been walked.

Until.

Until he tripped and broke his leg. Everybody said it served him right.

Crow had to walk on crutches for a long time and the other birds laughed at him, especially the doves. What's funnier than a bird flying with a crutch under one wing?

Now Crow was ashamed for having been so foolish. He had learned his lesson. As soon as his leg healed he would go back to walking the way he always had and leave dove walking to doves.

The day came. Crow's leg was healed. He put down his crutch and tried to take a crow step. He stumbled. He took another crow step. He stumbled again. Crow could not believe it. He had forgotten how to walk like a crow!

All that day Crow put one leg in front of the other, but as hard as he tried, he couldn't remember how to walk like a crow. And he was afraid to walk like a dove because he might trip and break his leg again. If he couldn't remember how to walk like a crow and was afraid to walk like a dove, the only thing he could do was hop.

And crows have been hopping ever since.

CHAPTER NINE

The Grand Parade

EVEN IF THE CREATURES were dissatisfied with how God created them, God was very proud of his world. He decided that he would look at everything again before he began the last job, creating people.

"Satan!" he called.

There was no answer.

"Satan!" he called again. Still no answer.

"Did you need something, God?" Sara asked.

"Well, yes, Sara. Yes, I do."

"Anything I might be able to help you with?"

"Maybe you can. But, would you happen to know where Satan is?"

Sara hesitated. "Uh, well, maybe." She wished God hadn't asked because she didn't want to tell him, but how could she lie to God?

"Well, where is he?"

"Uh, he's not here."

God sighed from within the light. "I know that, Sara."

"Yes, sir. I know you do. Uh, well, well, I'm confused, God."

"Confused about what?"

"You're God, right?"

"Right."

"So, if you're God, which you are, then you know everything. Why are you asking me where Satan is?"

The light glowed a rosy color and Sara thought that was a smile. "Good question," he responded. "Sara, I'm not sure if I know everything. Moon and the creatures on earth have been surprising me by doing things I hadn't thought of. Maybe there are things that are as mysterious to me as I am to the creatures. And that's all right. Wouldn't you rather have a God who can learn things?"

"If you can learn things, that means you have to listen, doesn't it?"

The light turned a deep rose. "Yes. Yes, it does. One cannot learn if he does not listen. So, I'm listening. Where's Satan?"

"He's at his school."

"School? What are you talking about?"

"I haven't been there, so I'm not sure. But it seems like he's teaching a lot of the angels how to do things."

"Such as?"

"Uh, things like, well, you know, things."

"Things like what?" God asked, getting impatient.

"Well, like how to clip an angel's wings when he's asleep so that when he wakes up and tries to fly, he can't. Or how to fly down to earth without your knowing. Things like that."

"I see," God said.

The light began to dim and Sara thought God was getting angry.

"So, what do you need me to do for you?" Sara asked quickly.

"Yes, yes. Of course," God responded, the light returning. "Forgive me, but your news about Satan and his school distresses me. But I will tend to him later. Today, however, I want to have a parade."

"A parade?" Sara asked, puzzled.

"Yes, I am almost finished creating, so I want all the creatures to line up and walk by so we can admire them. Would you get all the angels together to watch?"

Sara hesitated. "Are you sure that's a good idea? Some of the

angels like Satan and Alexander are not happy about this world you made. In fact, there are a lot of angels who don't like your world."

"Nonsense!" God responded. "There is nothing for them to be unhappy about. Go. Tell them there is going to be a parade and I want them to see what I have done." Sara sent messengers throughout heaven with God's message. Many of the angels were excited. They had never been to a parade. Others were not pleased.

"I don't see why he makes such a big deal out of his world," Satan said. "Any of us could have made a world—if we had wanted to."

"I don't know about that," responded Gabriel. "We're not God."

Satan lowered his voice. "What if we are as powerful as God but don't know it? What if we have let him convince us that we are only angels but, in reality, we're gods, too?"

"Do you know what you're saying?" Gabriel was shocked.

"And what if it is true?" Satan whispered. "What if I'm right? What then?"

Gabriel didn't know what to think. "I think we should go before God misses us" was all he could say.

When all the angels were assembled, God said, "I have a special treat for you today. I am almost done with creation. I thought you might want to visit the world and see everything I have created." He paused, then added, "Those of you who haven't done so already."

Some of the angels tried to hide, but most were excited. Earth looked like a wonderful place with its colors and trees, plants, flowers, animals, birds, and fish.

God turned himself into a cape of rose petals and beckoned the angels to follow. The angels spread their wings and followed him down through space. The animals, creatures, trees, and all that lived on earth looked up in awe as the sky filled with winged angels dressed in robes with colors as soft as kindness. All the birds on earth flew up to meet them and escort them to earth.

God and the angels landed on the wide plains of Africa where

46

he turned himself into a mountain whose snow-covered peak reached toward the sun.

"Let the parade begin," God said. "Let my creatures present themselves so we may glory in your wonder and beauty."

All day the creatures walked past proudly. Having tried to be what they weren't, they now knew how wise God was. Monkeys were swinging on the necks of the giraffes, and dolphins were leaping over elephants while birds made nests in the manes of the lions.

As each creature walked by it shouted, "Thank you, God, for making me!"

"Thanks, God! I like being alive!"

Some creatures started singing, "Hallelujah! Praise God!"

When the parade was over, Sara said to God, "You did good."

"How did you think of all that?" Jennifer asked admiringly.

God didn't know what to say. "I don't know. Maybe it had something to do with being in the darkness for so long."

"What do you mean?" Aviva asked.

"Sometimes you need to stay in the darkness for a long time because of the magnitude of what you are going to create."

God would've said more but he happened to notice Satan talking to a snake. "Satan!" he called. "Get the angels back to heaven!"

Reluctantly Satan obeyed, and the angels spread their wings and followed him back to their abode above the sky.

God turned himself into a winged lion, but Sara could tell that something was bothering him.

"What's the matter?" she asked.

God shook his lion's mane. "I don't know. Things are not working out like I thought they would."

"You mean Satan?"

"Yes."

"I'm not surprised."

"You aren't?!" God exclaimed.

"No. The first time I saw him, something bothered me."

"What was it?"

"He seemed to think he was *too* special."

"You're right!" God agreed. "What do you think I should do about him?"

Sara thought for a minute. She wanted to tell God to turn him into a rock and throw him to the other side of infinity and make *her* God's new assistant. But from the way God was talking to her and asking her opinion, she wondered if that was what she was already. She just didn't have the title. "I don't think you should do anything," she told God finally.

"Why not?"

"Because you don't know what to do."

God looked at her sharply, surprised by her words. "What— what do you mean?"

"Well, when you know what to do, you just do it. So, if you're wondering what to do, then maybe you should just keep on wondering until you don't wonder anymore."

God chuckled, but because he was now a lion, his chuckle was so loud and deep that it scared the green off the grass. And to this day, grass turns brown in the autumn and winter. That's because it's remembering the time God laughed like a lion.

"Would you like a ride back to heaven?" he asked Sara softly.

Sara's eyes got big. "Well, sure. I mean, if it's all right."

"Get on."

Sara climbed onto the winged lion. Her fingers gripped its black mane tightly as the lion flapped its wings. Sara laughed as the wind from the lion's wings blew gently in her face and she flew back to heaven on the back of God.

GENESIS 2:7: *And the Lord God formed the man from the dust of the earth and breathed into his nostrils the soul of being and the man became a living soul.*

. . . .

CHAPTER TEN

God Makes People

THE MORNING AFTER the parade God was awakened by Sara shouting frantically, "God! God! Wake up! Wake up!"

"What? What? What's wrong?"

"Some of the angels are flying down to the world and making fun of the animals."

"What!" God exclaimed, coming wide awake. He looked down at the world and saw Alexander talking to an elephant.

"What are you?" Alexander asked.

The elephant didn't answer.

Alexander laughed. "Can't talk. Can't think and can't fly, either. Too bad. If you were an angel, you could do all that and more."

The elephant, like all animals, understood it was being made fun of and its feelings were hurt.

God reached down and gathered the errant angels. They were back in heaven before they knew they were no longer on earth. "Just because you are special it does not mean you can make fun of others. You are the beings closest to me, and you cannot do anything that would make any creature think ill of me. Do you understand?"

The angels nodded, but God was not certain that they cared.

The angels didn't know it, but perhaps they were warning God about what was to come. People were going to be almost like angels because they would be the most special of all on earth. And they would know it, too. That was why God had created rocks and fleas and everything else first. Maybe if people remembered that everything else was in the world before they came along, then maybe they wouldn't think being special was the same as being better. God had a funny feeling it wasn't going to work out that way, though.

But his first problem was the angels. Some of them were not going to be very happy about the creation of people. He wasn't sure if the creatures and the elements were going to be pleased, either. So he decided to talk it over with them first.

Heaven thought it was a good idea. The bugs liked the idea because they would have somebody to bite besides the animals. The trees were opposed because they knew people were going to cut them down. The rocks and the moss on the rocks said they didn't care. They weren't going anywhere and weren't going to be doing anything for eternity anyway. Almost everything in creation told God to do what he thought best.

Then it was time to talk with the angels. Michael and his clan were first.

"We are not happy about these people," Michael began, "but if this is your desire, we will follow your wishes and do everything you want us to." Before he could continue, however, Alexander interrupted.

"Whatever gave you the idea of making humans? You don't need to do that! You can put us on earth. We will take care of it. These humans are not going to do that. Creation was perfect until now. To be frank, God, I don't think you know what you're doing anymore. Satan would make a better god than you."

God was disgusted. It was all he could do to mumble, "Get out of my sight!" To his surprise, Alexander disappeared.

"What happened?" God asked. "Where did he go?"

"You have to be careful how you say something," Sara offered. "Words are actions."

"Oh. I forgot," God said, embarrassed.

"God," Michael began. "I am sorry for the behavior of a member of my clan. Please forgive me."

God was pleased by Michael's words and made him Guardian of Prayers. "It will be your job to bring the people's prayers to me."

The next angels to come before God were Labbiel and his clan. Labbiel overheard what happened to Alexander and told his people, "Yo! Listen up! Whether you like it or not, we're going to get one hundred percent behind God's program. Anyway, you know God. He's going to do whatever he wants, anyway, so let me do all the talking."

Before God had a chance to ask Labbiel how he and the angels liked their new no-press robes, Labbiel said, "Yo! I think this idea of creating humans is fantastic! My clan and I would like to be the attendants of these humans."

God was so pleased he changed Labbiel's name to Raphael the Rescuer and made him the Angel of Healing.

To this day Raphael and his clan keep records of all the healing herbs on earth.

Throughout the morning God talked with the angels.

Jennifer said she had to think about it and would get back to him. Moe didn't have an opinion, and Aviva didn't care what God did as long as he didn't do it to her.

The Angel of Love liked the idea because people would be full of love.

"Not so," put in the Angel of Truth. "Love can only exist where there is truth, and these humans will do nothing but tell lies."

"I disagree," said the Angel of Justice. "They will want a world in which everything is fair. When you put love and truth together you have justice."

The Angel of Peace shook her head. "I wish it were going to be that way, but it is not. I am so afraid that these humans are going to try and solve all their problems through fighting and wars."

After God listened to all the angels, he was left alone. He turned himself into darkness and thought for a long time about all that the creatures and the angels had told him. They were right, he concluded. People were probably going to do all the evil things they had said—and more. But—but, wouldn't they also do good things?

God wanted to believe they would, wanted to believe that they would do more good than evil, but he was not sure. He had no choice but to create them and then see.

The time had come.

The angels gazed upward as the long, rippling red ribbons of light emerged from the darkness. The ribbons began moving as if dancing in a wide circle, slowly at first, then faster and faster until they were only a blur. The blur slowed to a spinning and then stopped. Instead of ribbons, a woman stood before them with skin as dark as wonder, hair as long as hope and white as fear. She was dressed in a robe as soft as tears and red as sorrow.

"I want Gabriel," she called.

"Here I am," Gabriel answered, flying immediately from the crowd.

"Bring me dust from the four corners of the Earth," she told him.

Gabriel flew to the north corner. When he reached down to pick up a handful of dust, Earth moved away and would not let him take any.

"That's strange," Gabriel muttered. Then he shrugged. "Maybe the Earth in the north is shy."

He flew to the east corner and reached down to pick up a handful of dust. The same thing happened. Earth moved away and would not let any of her dust be taken.

"What's going on?" Gabriel asked, a little concerned. Then he shrugged. "Oh, well. Maybe the Earth in the east is not feeling well."

He flew to the south. The same thing happened. He flew to the west. The result was the same.

"Why won't you do what God wants?" he asked Earth, exasperated.

"These humans are going to be disobedient and God will put

a curse on them *and* me, even though I didn't do anything. If God wants to use my dust to create these beings, she must gather it herself."

Gabriel flew back to heaven and he was angry. "I flew all over the world for nothing. Earth wouldn't even give me the time of day, not to mention any dust. What did I get out of it? Nothing but six sore wings and shoulders that ache like you wouldn't believe. You're God. You don't have shoulders. What do you care? Do you realize how hard it is to flap six wings at the same time and get them all flapping together? I was flying over the Himalayas and wing number three got a cramp in it and I almost fell out of the sky and stabbed myself on the top of one of them mountains. You did all the other creating by yourself. How come you ask for help now? And anyway, what's the big deal about getting dust from the four corners of the Earth? The way Earth is acting, you better use whatever dust you can get from wherever you can get it."

Gabriel paused and God spoke quickly. "Enough! You do carry on, don't you?"

The angel chuckled. "It was fun, too. But seriously, God, why do you need dust from the four corners?"

"When humans die they are going to turn to dust. Suppose someone who lived in the east died in the west. The Earth in the west might say, 'You didn't come from here so I will not receive your body.' If people are created with dust taken from each corner, the Earth will have to receive the body regardless of where the person dies.

"Also, the dust of each corner is a different color—black, white, yellow, and red. Because humans will be made from all four mixed together, no one can ever say that he is better than anyone else."

Gabriel shook his head. "That's what you hope. I've got a feeling about these humans and it's not a good one."

God did not hear his last remark because she had flown down to Earth and, quicker than the pause between a heartbeat, scooped dust from the four corners. Then she began work.

It was difficult to make the various body parts, to figure out where they should go, and then make them fit. The liver wanted to be up next to the eyeball and the stomach insisted on being between the toes while the lungs wanted to hang off the earlobes and the heart wanted to be on the tip of the nose so everybody could see it go *bumpity-bump.* It took a while but God eventually persuaded the organs to go where she wanted them to.

The angels were looking down from heaven and watching the form take shape.

"Kind of looks like us," Aviva said.

"Except where are its wings?" Moe wanted to know.

"Looks kind of big, doesn't it?" Meshabber added.

The figure looked finished to them, but God was still working.

"What's he doing?" Moe asked.

"She," Sara corrected him.

"She, he. Maybe he can switch back and forth all the time, but he shouldn't expect me to. I don't care what he looks like. She's a he and he's a she and that's that. So, what's he doing now?"

Sara was baffled, too. "God?" she called. "Aren't you finished with your creature?"

"Not quite," God responded.

"What else do you need to do?"

"Make the souls."

"The souls?" the angels whispered to each other, and then shrugged. "What's that?"

"It is my breath," God answered. "I blow a little of me into each human being. Just as I fill the world, the soul fills the body. As I see everything but cannot be seen, the soul sees but is not seen. As I guide the world, the soul guides the body. Just as I am pure, so is the soul, and just as I live in secret, so does the soul."

"Sounds deep," Moe commented.

God smiled. "Well, I suppose it is. You see, each person will have five souls—the Soul of Blood, the Soul of Wind, the Soul of Breath, the Soul of All Life, and the Individual Soul."

"Why so many?" Sara wanted to know.

"Each one has a different job. The Soul of Blood is in charge of the physical life because the life of a person is in the blood.

"The Soul of Wind fills the body and keeps it warm so people won't die in their sleep, unless they are very ill.

"The Soul of Breath is the spiritual aroma. When people meet each other they will be able to smell and see if a person wants to do them good or evil.

"Then there is the Soul of All Life. It makes the bones and muscles and cells come to life. The Soul of Life also has another job. Every night after I decide who will live another day and who will not, the Soul of Life will go to heaven and get the next day's allotment of new life for that person. However, on its way to and from heaven it will have all kinds of adventures with the other Souls of All Life and the Angels of Dreams will take these and weave them into people's sleep.

"Last will be the Individual Soul, that part of myself I give each person to care for."

God made all the souls of all the people that will ever be and put them in a storehouse in the seventh heaven. (There is a separate storehouse for the souls of all the animals.) When a woman is going to have a baby, the Angel of the Night, Lailah, takes the tiny seed of the baby to God.

She will look at it and say, "Oh, yes. That's Abdul." Or "That's Rochelle," or whoever. Then God decides if the person will be tall or short, rich or poor, fat, skinny, or whatever. Everything about the person's life is determined except whether he or she will live a good life or evil one. God has no control over that, only the person.

After making these decisions, God turns to the Angel of Souls. "Bring me the soul of Jose," or whoever. She describes what Jose looks like so the angel won't bring back the soul of a Jose who isn't supposed to be born until the year 9711. But the Angel of Souls always brings the right one. Then God tells the soul, "Enter this person."

The soul hesitates. "I am holy and pure and part of you," she says. "Why do you want me to live in a body?"

"Do not worry," God reassures her. "I created you to live in a human body." But the soul does not want to live in a body, so God forces it into the body. Then she appoints two angels to watch over the mother in case the soul tries to escape.

Each of us has two guardian angels. One represents the good we want to do. The other represents the evil. On Judgment Day the two angels will stand before God. One will tell her the good you did. The other will talk about all you did that you shouldn't have and all you could have but didn't. But as long as the soul is inside the mother, the angels feel how lonely and afraid she is, and they put a light above her so she can see from one end of the world to the other.

When it is almost time for the soul to enter the world, the angels take her out of the mother and show her all the places in the world where she will live and where she will die and where she will be buried. Then the angels return her to the mother's womb.

Finally, the day comes and the hour comes. The baby is ready to be born. "It is time for you to come into the world," the angels announce to the soul.

"Why? I like it in here!" the soul shouts back.

The angels reply, "You were made against your will and you will be born against your will. One day you will die against your will, and on the Day of Judgment you will stand before God and, against your will, have to account for your life."

"So what?" the soul shouts back. "It's warm and cozy in here and I'm not coming out."

The angels have no choice. The soul must come into the world. The angels look at each other and wink. Then, they tickle the soul. She starts giggling and can't stop and before she knows it, she is in the world. When the baby feels the cold air, the soul forgets everything she saw and learned about where she will live and die and be buried.

Thus we are born, laughing and crying.

GENESIS 2:8–9: *And the Lord God planted a garden in Eden, to the east, and there put the man he had formed. And from the ground, the Lord God caused to sprout every tree that was delightful and desirable to see and good to eat and the tree of life in the middle of the garden and the tree of the knowledge of good and evil.*

∙∙

CHAPTER ELEVEN

God Creates Adam

THE FIRST PERSON was born fully grown and he was called Adam, which means "man." He was twenty-one years old and was the largest person who ever lived. When he stood his head reached into heaven. His skin was as black as mystery and his smile as sweet as knowledge. The angels gasped when they saw him and wondered if he was another god.

After the angels finished admiring him, God showed him the earth. "I want you to decide which parts of the world will be for people and which for animals and in which parts the two will live close by each other."

Adam took a long time and God was pleased that he approached the task with such seriousness. Maybe, just maybe, these humans were going to be all right.

Then God brought him to Gan Eden—the Garden of Eden. She showed him the trees heavy with fruits, flowers whose blooms never wilted, and streams flowing with water as cold and clear as winter. Every animal that ever was also lived in Gan Eden, but they were as tame as daffodils because this was paradise.

God paused when they came to the center of Gan Eden where a large tree, aching with fruit, grew. "This is the Tree of the Knowledge of Good and Evil," God told Adam. "You may eat any fruit in the garden except that on this tree."

"Why can't I eat this fruit?" Adam wanted to know. "It looks really good."

God looked at Adam sharply. There was a different tone in Adam's voice, as if he was questioning her. "Do not be deceived. If you eat this fruit you will die."

Adam was confused. "What's die?"

"It means you will cease to exist. Do you understand?"

Adam was not sure he did, but he sensed that God wanted him to say yes, so he did.

"I made everything here just for you," God continued. "You are the caretaker of my world. If you harm it or destroy anything in it, no one, not even I, will be able to fix it."

"I understand," Adam said. But he didn't.

Many angels had flown down to Gan Eden, curious for a closer look at this creature who looked like them but was not. With so many angels around, God thought this might be a good time to teach Satan a lesson.

"Satan. Come. How would you like to have a contest with Adam?"

Satan chuckled. "It wouldn't be fair. I'm an angel, the highest-ranking angel. I know almost as much as you do."

"True," God agreed. "But maybe Adam knows something you don't."

Satan scoffed. "Impossible!"

"But what if he does?"

Satan shook his head and laughed again. "It's not possible, but let's have your contest. But let's make the game interesting. If I win, I get to become god. How about it?"

"And if you lose?"

Satan hesitated. He hadn't thought about that. "Well, I . . . I don't know."

"If you lose, you bow down to Adam."

"That'll be the day. So, what's the contest?"

"The animals will walk past you. As they do, tell me each one's name."

"Animals don't have names," Satan said confidently.

"Of course they do," God responded. "Everything has a name. Even Adam knows that."

"You really think this human is smarter than I am, don't you?" Satan retorted angrily. "I'm hurt and insulted you think more of this human than you do me."

"Then prove me wrong," God returned.

"Bring on the animals!" Satan announced.

The first animal was an elephant.

"Butterfly!" Satan said.

Next came a gorilla.

"Centipede!"

Then came a cat.

"Alligator!"

All day the animals walked past and all day Satan called out wrong names. Finally, when the last animal went by, Satan turned to God, his chest puffed out. "How did I do?" he asked, certain he had called every one by its right name. The angels who had been attending Satan's school applauded and cheered.

"Right on, Satan!" they shouted. "Right on!"

When the tumult died down, God said quietly, "You didn't get one right."

"What?" Satan exclaimed. "What do you mean? What do you *mean*? That can't be. I don't believe you. You're lying!"

Every angel, every animal, every flower and tree, every blade of grass, every bird and fish held its breath. The world stopped turning on its axis. The chariot carrying Sun up the roof of heaven stopped in its tracks. Satan heard a silence more fearful than any ever heard. He looked around. Nothing moved, but the eyes of every creature, the petals of every flower, and each blade of grass all stared at him.

He looked away. He couldn't believe that in his anger he had dared call God a liar. Afraid of what God might do to him, he turned to her. "Forgive me. I did not mean that. You are truth and are incapable of lying. My disappointment at my poor performance caused me to lose my head."

"Watch Adam," God said calmly, not mollified by Satan's apology.

The animals paraded past again. On the soul of each, God had imprinted its name and given Adam the power to read it. So, as the animals walked by, Adam called them by name. Each one stopped and bowed to Adam in acknowledgment.

When the procession of animals ended, Satan was furious. It was time for him to bow to Adam. He knew God had tricked him, but he couldn't figure out how.

God stared at Satan. Satan stared back.

"I won't do it," Satan said finally. "You can do to me whatever you want to, but I will not bow to this creature of yours. And I do not want to be your assistant! I want my own world, a world where there will be no creature named Adam, a world where I will rule, I and my angels."

"Right on!" shouted Satan's angels. "Right on!"

God stared at Satan and experienced a sadness she feared would never go away. How had she been so misguided as to make him her assistant? Or had being her assistant changed him? Whatever the reason, she had failed. But how could that be? How could *God* fail?

The angels waited for her to speak or do something. She would not do either until she understood how and why she had failed. No one knew how much time passed because a thousand years was scarcely a minute in that realm occupied by God and the angels. She waited until finally she knew.

Nothing had gone wrong. Failure was also part of creation. Satan would always be God's assistant, just not in the way she had first thought.

"Very well," God said at last. "You shall have your world. Just as Tehom has her world beneath the waters, you shall have yours beneath the earth. From there you may devise tests for the souls of the humans, but whatever you do will only bring them closer to me. Of that I have no doubt."

Satan smiled. "We'll see about that, God. We'll see."

Many angels were sorry Satan was going to leave. He was so much fun and always had great ideas of things to do. God was dismayed to see how many gathered around to wish him good-bye and good luck.

"God, can I go with Satan?" an angel asked suddenly.

"Me, too."

"Yes, I would like to be with him."

"So would I."

Angel after angel after angel shouted the same wish.

"Think carefully," God warned them. "If you go to the world below, you can never return to this one."

"We understand," they said. "We understand."

Sara was shocked. "But if you leave, you will never again be in God's presence."

"We understand," the angels with Satan answered with one voice.

Sara shook her head sadly. "No. No, you do not."

"It's all right, Sara," God comforted her. "It's all right."

Without another word, God grabbed Satan and the myriad of angels who wanted to be with him and flung them as deep into the earth as she had put Tehom in the sea.

GENESIS 2:18—20:   *And the Lord God said, It is not good that the man is alone. I will make a companion for him. And from the earth the Lord God formed every beast of the field and every bird of the heavens and he brought them to the man to see what he would call each and whatever the man called a creature's soul that was its name. And the man called names to all the creatures and the birds of the heavens and to all the beasts of the field but the man did not find a companion.*

∙∙

CHAPTER TWELVE

God Creates Woman

GOD HAD SCARCELY finished with Satan and his angels when he heard a strange sound coming from Adam. God looked at him and saw water coming from his eyes and trickling down his face.

"What's wrong?" God asked. "Did your eyes break? They were almost as tricky to make as figuring out how to get teeth to grow from the jaw."

"I don't know what's wrong," Adam said. "When I was naming the animals, a funny feeling came over me."

"What was it like?"

Adam thought for a minute. "Well, I started wishing I was one of the animals."

"You wished what?" God asked, a little hurt.

"I don't want to *be* an animal," Adam hastened to explain, wiping his eyes. "But as the animals paraded past I noticed that all of them had one of their kind to be with. I don't have anyone. In all of creation there is no one who walks and talks and looks like me."

God smiled. She had wondered how long before Adam noticed that he was alone.

"You're lonely," God told him. "Come. It is time."

64

God kneeled in the dust and began making a companion for Adam. Adam peered over her shoulder, watching every move.

"Uh, pardon me, God, but what's that white hard stuff you're making?"

"Bones."

"I don't have that inside me, do I?"

"Sure."

"Yuck!"

Adam watched a while longer. "Uh, pardon me, God. What are those disgusting looking things you're putting in?"

"Kidney, gallbladder, pancreas, intestines, stomach, lungs, and spleen."

"I know I don't have any of that in me. Right?"

"Wrong."

"Gross!"

Adam watched for a while longer. "Uh, pardon me, God."

"Whatever it is, you probably have it, too," God said impatiently. "There're a few things the woman will have that you don't and a few things you have that she won't, but for the most part, you're alike."

Adam was so disgusted at seeing the organs and all that went into making a human being that he almost threw up. Is it any wonder he didn't appreciate his wife? But neither Adam nor God had ever been married. They didn't know that love needs mystery.

Lilith was her name. She was as tall as Adam and as beautiful as he was handsome. She would have been a wonderful wife if Adam had known how to be a partner. He didn't. Because he was the first human and because God had shown him the entire universe as if it were her gift to him, Adam thought Lilith, too, had been created just for him.

As soon as God breathed the soul into Lilith and she opened her eyes, Adam said, "Come here, woman, and give my shoulders a rub. They ache a little bit."

Lilith narrowed her eyes. "Who are you?" she said, staring at him.

"I'm your husband. You're supposed to do what I say."

"And who said that?"

Adam started to say God, but God shook her head. "I didn't tell you that. You came up with that foolish idea all by yourself."

"I did!" Adam declared.

"Why can't we do what each other says?" Lilith asked, seeking a compromise.

"You mean, I should do what you say to do?"

"Well, some of the time. Why not?"

Adam was confused. That sounded reasonable, but it made him uncomfortable. "Well, because . . ." He didn't know what to say.

"Because what?" Lilith prompted.

"Just because!" he snapped, exasperated. "Now, give me a back rub."

Lilith shook her head. "First, I have no idea what a back rub is, and second, I don't like it when you speak to me that way. God made us equal."

"But I was first!"

God shook her head. "If I had known you were going to act like this, you would have been last," she said sadly.

Lilith began walking away. "I cannot stay if this is how you're going to be."

"Where're you going?" Adam wanted to know.

"Away from you."

"You can't do that!" Adam shouted.

"I can and I will."

And she did.

Adam was furious! How dare she not do what he told her to. How dare she leave him alone. God had created her to be with him!

You would not believe the stories Adam and, thereafter, other men told about Lilith. They said she went to the center of the earth and married Satan. If a man tripped while walking along a road, it was Lilith who tripped him. If a man woke up sleepy, it was because Lilith had taken his soul during the night. If a baby died, men said Lilith killed it.

God was saddened by how Adam treated Lilith and the stories he told about her. It made her even sadder when others believed the stories and made up ones of their own about her.

Nobody knows what happened to Lilith.

Except that she was very alone.

GENESIS 2:21–25: *And the Lord God caused a deep sleep to fall on the man and he slept. And the Lord God took one of his sides and he shut up the place with flesh. And the Lord God built up the side which he had taken from the man into a woman and brought her to the man. And the man said, This time it is bone of my bones and flesh of my flesh. This will be called a woman because from a man she was taken. Thus a man shall leave his father and mother and be lovingly devoted to his wife and they shall be one flesh. And both of them were naked, the man and his wife, and they were not ashamed.*

· ·

CHAPTER THIRTEEN

Adam Marries

GOD HAD A PROBLEM. Adam was still lonely and needed a companion. God wasn't sure he deserved a second chance, but that was her fault. She shouldn't have let him watch her make Lilith. Maybe it had been a mistake, also, to make Lilith from the dust as she had Adam. Maybe if God made the second woman from a part of the man, he would treat her as he would want to be treated.

God put Adam to sleep, took flesh from his side, and shaped it into a woman. God paused, remembering again how Adam had treated Lilith, and decided to make women smarter because they were going to have to deal with men all their lives.

Adam awoke and a beautiful Woman lay beside him. This time he knew better than to ask her to do what he said. Now he saw the Woman as separate from him and as an offering. And he saw that he was separate and an offering, too.

The Woman was so darkly beautiful her skin looked to be as soft as a flower's whisper. "Flesh of my flesh," Adam said.

Taking her hand, Adam took her through the garden, showing her the flowers and bushes, telling her the names of the animals and birds. They walked slowly, stopping to taste the sweet flesh of the fruits—plums and melons and grapes. They ran through the tall grasses of the meadows and splashed in the waters of the cold streams.

The last thing Adam showed her was the Tree of the Knowledge of Good and Evil. God could not hear what he said, but Adam talked for a long time, gesturing toward the tree as he did so.

God was pleased. "Adam is treating this wife much better. Maybe everything will be all right."

"When do I get to meet God?" the Woman asked.

The question surprised Adam. The Woman was smarter than he had thought. "I—I don't know," he said with a nervous laugh. "God didn't say anything about you meeting her."

"But God sees you every day."

"Well, yes, but that's because there is so much God needs to teach me."

"Isn't God going to teach me?"

Adam laughed that nervous laugh again. "God teaches me and I teach you. Everything I've told you is what God told me. You know as much as I do now."

Reluctantly, the Woman agreed, but she still didn't understand why God wouldn't talk to her, too. The Woman didn't know she could have talked to God without asking Adam first. Too, Adam could have introduced her to God, if he had wanted to. But he didn't. If the Woman didn't know as much as he did, then she would always need him. She would always be dependent on him. That is what Adam thought.

God's next-to-final act was the wedding of Adam and the Woman. God made a wedding dress from sunlight and birdsongs. She braided the Woman's hair and adorned it with angel's wishes. As God led the Woman to the marriage canopy, the angels played on

musical instruments and danced. Then God sang the marriage ceremony in flawless Hebrew.

With the joining of Adam and the Woman, creation was complete.

Quietly, God returned to the ribbon shape and wafted back to heaven.

"Welcome home," Sara greeted him.

"Thanks. Well, I'm done, Sara. My world is almost complete."

"It's a beautiful world, God."

"Yes. It is, isn't it?"

"So, what else do you need to create?"

"Shabbat. The day of rest."

And so God rested from all the work he had done and he contemplated himself and the infinite universe and he was refreshed and renewed.

GENESIS 3:1–6: *And the serpent was more crafty than any beast of the field which the Lord God made and the serpent said to the woman, "Is it possible that God said, 'Do not eat from any tree in the garden?'"*

And the woman said to the serpent, "From the fruit of any tree of the garden we may eat, but of the fruit of the tree in the middle of the garden God said, 'Do not eat from it and do not touch it or you will die.'" And the serpent said to the woman, "Nonsense! You will not die. God knows that on the day you eat your eyes will be opened and you will be like God and you will know good and evil." And the woman saw that the tree was good for food and it was a delight to the eyes and that it was desirable as a means to make one wise and she took from its fruit and she ate.

• •

CHAPTER FOURTEEN

The Snake

THE WOMAN LOVED Gan Eden and especially all the strange and wonderful creatures who lived there. There was the Shamir, a worm as large as an ear of corn, which could cut through anything. Adam told her that God created it for one purpose—to cut the massive stones for building the Temple in Jerusalem because no iron could be used in its construction. One of the Woman's favorite creatures was the Zabua. Made from a white drop, it had 365 different colors, one for each day of the year. She was not as fond of the Barnacle Goose, however. It was a goose that grew on trees. God must not have slept well the night before he made that.

The animals were happy the Woman lived there. She understood the language of every creature—birds and lions, butterflies and dolphins—and could speak to each in its language. It would probably be that way still if not for Snake. But it's not fair to blame it all on him. Adam and the Woman made their own mistakes.

In Gan Eden, Snake had legs and walked upright. He was as

tall as a camel and much better looking. Snake was also the smartest of all the creatures. He was so smart he didn't let Cat know how smart he was. Leviathan did not know how smart Snake was. He was as smart as Adam and the Woman, and he knew it. They didn't. Snake was as smart as God and knew that, too. So did God.

Snake was sitting on a limb high in the Tree of the Knowledge of Good and Evil, watching Adam and the Woman running through the tall grasses of the meadow.

"If I am as smart, if not smarter, than they are, why do they get to be humans and I have to remain a snake, albeit a very handsome one," he wondered aloud. The more Snake thought about it, the more unfair it seemed. The more unfair it seemed, the angrier he became. There had to be a way to even things up. He thought and he thought and he thought. He thought until he thought of a plan. And then he waited.

That afternoon God descended to earth in the form of butterflies, hundreds and hundreds of orange, yellow, blue, and white butterflies. They swarmed around Adam and lifted him into the air.

The Woman watched as the butterflies carried Adam into the sky and out of sight. She was overcome by a deep feeling of yearning, wishing that God liked her as much as he liked Adam, wishing God would show her something he had never shown Adam.

Snake had not been impressed by God's appearance as butterflies. He was getting bored with God showing up as a woman one day and a ribbon of light the next. Pick a shape and stick with it! Snake wanted to tell him, her, or whatever.

Snake looked at the Woman, who stood near the Tree of the Knowledge of Good and Evil, staring wistfully into the sky after God and Adam. He knew what she was feeling because it was an emotion he felt, too. And he knew this was the moment he had been waiting for.

Swiftly Snake climbed down and sat on the lowest branch of the tree.

"Good afternoon," Snake said politely.

The Woman was startled by the unexpected voice and looked away from the now empty sky, bewildered until she saw Snake perched on the branch. "Good afternoon, Snake."

"Adam's off on a business trip with God again, huh?"

She nodded, her eyes tearing.

"*Tsk. Tsk. Tsk*," went Snake. "If I were Adam, I wouldn't go on a business trip and leave you all alone."

The Woman blushed. "That's a nice thing to say, but I'm fine. They'll be back before night."

Snake jumped down from the tree and walked over to the Woman. She sat down so that they would be at eye level. "What do you think of Gan Eden?"

Her eyes brightened. "Oh, I love it. It is so beautiful!"

Snake agreed. "Yes, it is, isn't it? What have God and Adam told you about it?"

"Oh, everything. The names of all the animals and the names of all the places where our descendants will live. And much, much more."

"I'm glad. I like to check on God from time to time to make sure he, she, or whoever is doing a good job." Snake chuckled, then continued. "For instance, what did God tell you about the trees here?"

"Adam told me God said we could eat the fruit of any tree except this one." She pointed to the tree behind them. "However, not only can't we eat the fruit of this tree, we can't even touch it."

"And why is that?" Snake asked, all innocence.

"Because we will die." She wasn't sure what that was, but it didn't sound good.

Snake smiled to himself. He had the opening he needed. God hadn't said anything to Adam about not touching the tree. Maybe Adam added that little detail or maybe the Woman put it in, thinking she was doing the right thing. Wherever it came from, Snake carped the diem. "I knew it!" he exclaimed. "I knew it!"

"Knew what?"

"I knew that God couldn't be trusted to tell the truth."

The Woman was shocked. "You can't talk like that about God."

Snake chuckled. "Oh, it's all right. We're like brothers, or brother and sister, or brother and ribbons, or brother and butterflies, or—"

"I understand," the Woman said. "What're you trying to say?"

"What I'm trying to say is that God and I know each other very well. So I do not speak out of disrespect but with knowledge. Come. Let me show you something."

Without warning, Snake pushed the Woman against the tree.

She shrieked as she felt her back touch the tree and jerked her body away from it. "Look what you've done," she said. "I'm going to die and it's all your fault." She began crying.

Snake smiled. He waited a moment. "So? Tell me. How do you feel?"

After a moment the Woman stopped crying. She touched her face and hair and arms. "I—I feel fine."

"You want to repeat that for me, and a little louder this time?"

"I—I feel fine!"

"That's what I thought you said. You touched the tree and you feel fine. In other words, you touched the tree and nothing happened. Your hair didn't fall out. Your teeth didn't rot. Your toenails didn't turn to peanut butter. You're still the same, right?"

The Woman nodded slowly. "I don't understand. Adam said God said that we would die."

"God doesn't want you to know the truth."

"What truth?"

"This truth: God knows that if you eat the fruit of this tree that you will be able to create and destroy just like him."

"I'll be like God?" the Woman asked, getting excited.

"Almost. You'll be as close to being like God as anything can be. There's something else, something God has not told Adam."

"What? Please tell me. I would love to know something Adam doesn't know."

"God created everything in a particular order. Each thing on earth has power over whatever was created before it. The very last thing God created has power over everything. What was created last?"

She blinked, then shook her head. "Well, I was, but—"

"But what? If you were created last, aren't you supposed to be the ruler of what came before you? And what came before you? Adam. All the creatures. Why is it that you can understand and speak with all the creatures in their language and Adam can't?"

"I never thought of that," the Woman responded. Then she shook her head. "No, what you say makes sense but it can't be right."

Snake knew better than to try and convince her. "You can believe me or not," he shrugged. "That's up to you. But let me tell you this, which is something else God hasn't told Adam. God is going to create another world. When he does, those people will have power over everything on this world—including you. Do you want to live with somebody from another world telling you what you can and can't do? It's bad enough with God doing it."

The Woman shook her head. "What can I do?"

"If you eat of the Tree of the Knowledge of Good and Evil, you will be like God, and then you can do whatever you want."

The Woman was tempted, but then shook her head. "I don't know. God was very definite about not eating the fruit of this tree. I don't want to disobey God."

Snake acted as if he hadn't heard her and nonchalantly reached up and shook a branch of the tree. Pieces of fruit fell to the ground. Snake picked one up and bit into it. The sweet juices were cool in his throat. "Ahhhhh! That's good fruit. And look! *Ta da!!* I'm not dead, whatever that is."

The Woman stared at Snake. He seemed to be the same. He picked up another piece of fruit. She stared at its curved flesh and felt like she could taste it already. Snake held it out to her. She reached for it, then pulled back her hand. But it looked sooooo good. Maybe if she took only a little bite. Just enough to know what it tasted like but not enough that she would die.

The Woman didn't know what to do. God has said . . . but she touched the tree and nothing had happened to her. Snake had eaten the fruit and nothing had happened to him. "What should I do?" she said, agonized.

"What could be the harm in taking just a tiny bite, just to see what it tastes like. You probably won't even like it," Snake suggested.

He was right. What could happen if she took just a teeny-tiny-teenichy bite? Slowly, she raised the fruit, brought it to her lips, and bit the outside skin. She picked at it lightly with her tongue, then stopped and waited, holding her breath.

"You're OK," Snake reassured her. "Still got your hair and your teeth and"—he counted quickly—"all your fingers and toes."

She let out her breath and laughed, embarrassed. She was still here. The sweet aftertaste of the fruit lingered on her tongue. Its juices were so thick they stuck to her fingers. She licked her fingers, then took another nibble. The thick syrup of the fruit was as cool and sweet in her mouth as tomorrow that never comes. Quickly she ate the rest.

"That was good!" she exclaimed. She burped and wiped her mouth. She had disobeyed God, but so what? God had not told the truth. In fact, God had not told her anything. How did she know if God had actually said what Adam said he said?

"Guess what I just did?" she said to a butterfly flitting past.

The butterfly continued as if it had not heard her. That's odd, the Woman thought. Butterflies always stopped to talk to her.

A squirrel scampered down a tree. "Hi!" the Woman called. "Guess what I just did?"

The squirrel squawked at the Woman and ran away. What is the matter with Squirrel? she wondered. Just that morning he had sat on her shoulder and taught her about the many kinds of nuts.

As she walked through the garden, it seemed that the animals no longer knew her. Deer always walked beside her, but now they bounded away as she came near. The birds that taught her songs flew out of the trees as she walked beneath.

"What's the matter?" the Woman cried out. The animals said nothing. Or were they speaking and she could no longer understand them? Were the animals shunning her because she had disobeyed God and eaten the fruit?

Something had changed. Where before she had known only happiness, where before her heartbeat had been as light as air, now it beat with the heaviness of sorrow and regret. Was this what God had meant by death?

What was she going to do? God and Adam would be angry with her. Maybe God would be so angry he would send her away. She looked around to ask Snake what he thought she should do, but he had vanished. It was almost as if he had never been there.

She had to do something. She didn't want to be sent away. God would then make another wife for Adam, one better than her. She knew what she had to do and she would have to do it as soon as Adam returned, do it before he realized.

. . . and she gave also to her husband with her and he ate. And the eyes of both of them were opened and they knew they were naked and they sewed fig leaves together and made themselves aprons.

••

CHAPTER FIFTEEN

The Woman, Adam, and the Fruit

THE THOUGHT HAD BARELY completed itself before she looked up and saw the sky filled with butterflies. God was bringing Adam back. The Woman ran to the Tree of the Knowledge of Good and Evil, and picked a fruit from one of its limbs.

God set Adam gently on the ground and the butterflies filled the sky, then disappeared as God returned to heaven. The Woman ran to meet Adam, threw her arms around his neck, and kissed him deeply on the lips.

"Is something wrong?" Adam asked, pulling away from her.

"Why, no," she said, wide-eyed. "What makes you think that?"

"What was that you were just doing, putting your arms around me and pressing your lips against mine? You have never done anything like that."

The Woman hadn't thought about it, but Adam was right. She *hadn't* done anything like that before, before eating the fruit. She had to act quickly before Adam started asking more questions.

"How was your day?" she asked him.

He grinned. "Great! Wait until I tell you what God showed me today."

"Aren't you going to ask me how my day was?"

"Well, I assumed it was like all the other days. You talked to the animals and they talked to you and like that."

81

"Even better." She smiled. "I discovered a wonderful fruit. You won't believe how delicious it is."

Adam was puzzled. "I thought I had tasted all the fruits here."

The Woman shrugged. "There're so many trees and fruits. You probably missed a couple."

"Maybe," Adam muttered, but he wasn't sure.

"Come on. Close your eyes."

Adam smiled, deciding to play along with her.

"Open wide."

As Adam opened his mouth, the Woman took the fruit from behind her back and put it in his mouth.

"Now, bite!"

Adam bit into the fruit and chewed slowly. "That's wonderful!" he exclaimed. "That's the best fruit I have ever eaten." He opened his eyes. "What is it?"

The Woman pointed to the tree and the fruit on the ground.

Adam could not believe what he was looking at. "It can't be. You didn't. I didn't."

"It is. You did and I did," the Woman responded simply.

Adam shook his head. "No. You wouldn't do that." He chuckled nervously. "No. You wouldn't disobey God. Stop playing with me. What is this fruit for real and where did you get it?"

"What does it look like, Adam?" the Woman repeated.

Adam was annoyed. "It *looks* like the fruit of the Tree of the Knowledge of Good and Evil. But you know what will happen if we eat that fruit and I know you have more sense than that."

"I do, but God said we shouldn't touch the tree, either. Well, I touched it and nothing happened to me. So, if nothing happened to me when I touched the tree, why should I believe something would happen to me from eating the fruit?"

There was a long pause. Tears came to Adam's eyes as he realized what had happened. "God didn't say anything about not touching the tree," he admitted finally.

"What?" the Woman exclaimed. "What do you mean?"

82

Adam looked away, ashamed. "God didn't say anything about not touching the tree," he repeated, his voice barely audible. "All God said was not to eat the fruit. I—I added the part about not touching it to make sure you wouldn't go near the tree."

The Woman was furious. "How could you? What made you think you couldn't tell me the truth? So, what else have you told me that God said but God really didn't say? If God talked to me, this would never have happened."

Adam did not have time to answer because something was happening. Adam and the Woman noticed that they were no longer looking over the tops of the clouds. Now they were looking at the tops of trees, no, into the trees, no, looking up at the trees, oh no!

Adam and the Woman looked at each other. Suddenly the world was bigger, much bigger, and they were smaller, much, much smaller.

"What's happened to us?" the Woman asked.

Adam shook his head. "I'm not sure. I think we shrank."

Then, they noticed something else. They were not wearing clothes. Adam blushed and didn't know what to say. The Woman pointed at him and started giggling. Adam pointed and giggled, too. It was as if they were seeing each other for the very first time and did not know where to look or not look, where to put their hands, or even if they should, or who the other was except a man and a woman, each naked before the other.

The Woman would have been content to gaze at Adam for a long time, to giggle and blush, to touch and wonder. But Adam was uncomfortable. He did not know what to do with all the feelings that arose in his body when he looked at her; he did not know what to do with all the feelings when he tried not to look at her.

He wanted to cover himself *and* her so he would not have to see her nor she him. He ran to pull leaves from a tree to cover their nakedness, but the tree pulled away from his hands. He ran to another tree. It, too, pulled away. The same happened with tree after tree. Finally he heard one tree say to another, "That is the man who disobeyed God. I will not let myself be touched by the hands of him who deceived God."

Only when Adam reached out to the fig tree did a tree not move. Because the fig tree did not turn away from Adam and the Woman, some think it was the fruit of the Tree of the Knowledge of Good and Evil. Others believe God asked the fig tree to be kind and give its leaves to them. But no one knows for sure what the fruit was because God feared that if anyone ever knew which fruit the Woman and Adam ate, no one would eat it ever again.

All that is known for sure is that the Woman and Adam wrapped themselves in skirts of fig leaves. Then they waited.

GENESIS 3:8–17, 20–21:   *And they heard the voice of the Lord God walking in the garden toward the cool of the day and the man and his wife hid from the Lord God among the trees of the garden. And the Lord God called to the man and said to him, Where are you? And the man said, I heard your voice in the garden and I was afraid because I am naked and I hid.*

And the Lord God said, Who told you that you are naked? Did you eat of the tree I commanded you not to eat from? And the man said, The Woman you gave to be with me, she gave me of the tree and I ate.

And the Lord God said to the Woman, What is this you have done? And the Woman said, The serpent seduced me and I ate.

And the Lord God said to the serpent, Because you did this, you are cursed beyond the cattle and all the beasts of the field. You shall travel on your belly and eat dust all the days of your life. I will put enmity between you and the Woman, between your descendants and her descendants, and they will beat your head and you shall hiss at their heel.

To the woman the Lord God said, I will greatly increase your pain and your labor in childbearing. In pain you will bear children. You shall run after your husband and he will rule over you.

To the man the Lord God said, Because you listened to the voice of your wife, and you ate from the tree of which I commanded you, saying Do not eat of it, cursed is the ground because of you. In grief you will eat from it all the days of your life. . . .

And the man called his wife's name Chavah because she was the mother of all the living. And the Lord God made for Adam and his wife garments of skin and he clothed them.

• •

CHAPTER SIXTEEN

God Confronts Adam, the Woman, and the Snake

GOD SAW ADAM and the Woman hiding behind some bushes and he laughed at how ridiculous they looked wearing leaves and tree branches. These humans were going to amuse him for a long time to come.

He was delighted. He wanted them to know almost as much as he did, but they had to choose that. Something so important was not God's to give but theirs to take. Snake and the Woman had played their roles perfectly.

God went to earth but this time he did not assume a form. He would be only a voice.

"Adam? Where are you?" God called.

Adam shivered at the sound of God's voice.

"What's the matter?" the Woman whispered.

"It's God!"

"I know, but you've never been afraid any other time he's called your name."

"But all the other times I hadn't done anything wrong."

The Woman shivered, too. "You're right."

"Didn't you hear what God asked?" Adam whispered.

"He wanted to know where you are."

"Yes," Adam agreed. "But this is God, remember? He knows where I am. So, if God wants to know where I am, he doesn't need to know where I am because he knows where I am."

"Is there a bottom line to this?" the Woman asked, exasperated.

"The bottom line is this: God wants me to ask myself, Where am I now compared to where I was yesterday? Yesterday my head floated above the clouds and I could rest my elbows on the tops of mountains. Today the clouds float high above my head and I cannot see the tops of the mountains. Yesterday I was naked and did not know it. Today I am wearing leaves to hide myself from your sight and my own. Yesterday we were caretakers of Gan Eden; today the creatures run from us and the trees turn their leaves away from my hands. God asked, 'Where are you?' I don't know anymore. I don't know."

The Woman looked at Adam. "That's true," she said softly.

"That's true. But don't you feel something today that you didn't feel yesterday?"

"Like what?"

"Well, when you look at me now, don't you feel as warm and sweet as the juice of the fruit? When you look at me now, doesn't your heart feel like it wants to laugh? When you look at me now, don't you want to touch me and feel my touch?"

Yes, Adam started to say, yes, yes, yes, but he didn't want those feelings. He was afraid they would control him, that she would control him. And if that happened, he did not think he would know who he was.

"Get away from me!" he snapped. "How dare you even speak to me after what you've done? We had everything. Now we have nothing."

"We have each other," the Woman pleaded.

Adam stared blankly at her, not knowing what she meant.

"Where are you?" came the voice of God again.

Adam and the Woman stepped from behind the bushes. "Uh, here we are, God."

"Why were you hiding behind the bushes?" God wanted to know.

"I'm naked, so I hid myself," Adam answered.

"And how do you know you're naked? Did you eat the fruit from the tree I told you not to?"

"It wasn't my fault," Adam spluttered angrily. "If you hadn't given me this Woman, it never would have happened. Things were fine as long as I was by myself. It was her idea. She had already eaten a piece of the fruit before I got home. Then, she tricked me into eating a piece. I trusted her and she deceived me."

God was stunned by Adam's words. They had not been part of his plan. He was afraid of what the Woman was going to say. "What is this you've done?" he asked her.

The Woman was stung and hurt that Adam had placed the

blame on her. What was she supposed to say now? What if God believed Adam and didn't believe her? "I didn't know what I was doing, God. Snake told me it would be all right and you know what a good talker he is."

Where before God had been proud of the Woman, now he was saddened by her words. Though what she said about Snake was true. That's why he didn't bother to ask Snake for his side of the story. Given the chance, Snake would have outtalked him.

Snake had been watching everything from deep within the leaves of the Tree of the Knowledge of Good and Evil.

"From this day forward, Snake, you will crawl on your belly in the dirt."

Thud! Snake who stood tall as a camel fell from the tree and onto the ground. He opened his mouth to protest, but before he could say a word, God continued.

"I take from you the power of language, but you will forever try to talk by flicking out your tongue. But people will mistake your silent speech and think you are trying to attack them, and human beings will hate you."

Snake lost his arms and legs, shrank in size, and his body coiled into circles of muscles upon circles of muscles. His head rested on the outer coil and was raised, the tongue flicking in and out, in and out, searching for the words that had been so readily his. Now no words came and the Woman shrank away from him and his tongue, flicking in and out, in and out.

"As for you, Woman, you shall give birth to children but it will be in great pain. And, of course, you will know death. And you will find out, in time, what that is.

"Adam, you will have to work for your food. You will dig it from the ground, the same ground to which you will return when you die."

Adam wept. "I do not understand."

"What's so hard to understand?" God wanted to know.

"Why are you so upset? Why are you doing all this to us? It is true that we disobeyed you, but it was the first time. Maybe we didn't know you really meant what you said. We're new at this business of being one of God's creatures. We deserve a second chance. We've learned our lesson."

"I am not punishing you because you disobeyed me," God explained. "I expected you would do that. You might even say I wanted you to."

"You did?" the Woman asked.

"That's why I couldn't talk to you. If I had told you directly not to eat the fruit, you wouldn't have disobeyed. I wanted you to be angry and upset with me, to feel a little rebellious."

"Oh."

"And, why do you think I put the Tree of the Knowledge of Good and Evil in the middle of the garden and then told you not to eat its fruit? If I hadn't wanted you to eat the fruit I would have hidden it deep in the garden where you would never find it. I was counting on you, especially, Woman. Why would I be showing Adam all the things in the world if I wanted you to stay here in the garden for eternity? No, I was counting on you to get him out of here so he can put to work all the wonderful things I've been showing him."

"Then I don't understand," the Woman replied. "If you wanted me to disobey you and eat the fruit, then why are you doing this to us?"

"When I asked you what happened, I didn't expect you to blame someone else. I expected you to take responsibility for what you did. I thought you would say, 'God, I did wrong. I disobeyed you and I'm sorry.' Instead, Adam blamed me and then blamed you. You blamed Snake, and if I had given him the chance, he would have probably blamed the tree. Your sin was not your disobedience. Your sin was not taking responsibility and asking forgiveness."

Adam looked at the Woman. "I'm sorry I tried to blame you," he told her.

"And I'm sorry I tricked you."

"I'm sorry I was afraid to tell you how beautiful you look to me."

"I forgive you," she replied.

Then Adam and the Woman turned to God and each said, "I'm sorry for what I did. I'm sorry that I did not take responsibility."

God nodded. "I accept your apologies. Because you have apologized, we can still be friends, but you cannot remain here any longer. Now, there is one last task you must perform, Adam."

"What is that?" he asked.

"You must look into the soul of the Woman and read her name alive."

Adam looked at her. She stared back at him, her eyes as bright as the sun's heart. He smiled, pleased that he was with her and she with him. Then he saw the words on her soul. "Chavah," he said. "You are named Chavah," which means "Mother of all Living."

Then Adam and Chavah made one last trip through the garden and said good-bye to all the flowers, plants, and trees, to all the animals and insects. For the last time, each one spoke to Chavah in their language and she understood.

God made clothes from animal skins for them and dressed them. Then he led them out of the garden.

"Look!" Chavah exclaimed, her eyes widening as the world stretched before her. "You know something, Adam?"

"What?"

"I think God played a joke on us."

"Oh?"

"Why just look! The world is more beautiful than the garden."

"Even though we will now know death?"

"And that is the reason why," she said. "That is the reason why."

Chavah and Adam walked into the world. Everything was going to be all right. When they were almost out of sight of Gan Eden, they turned around for one last look. All they saw was an angel with a flaming sword that turned continually in every direction barring their way back.

CHAPTER SEVENTEEN

God Returns to Heaven

GOD WAITED UNTIL they left. Then he took the form of a woman, this time a woman as pale as sorrow. She walked slowly through the garden. The birds flew above her head like a multicolored canopy. The creatures followed her as she looked at every petal on every flower and every leaf on every tree.

She had always known that they could not stay in the garden. She had not known how terribly much she would miss them and she cried.

It was a while before the tears ceased. Maybe a thousand years or so. Who knows? Finally, the tears ceased, however, and she changed into the red ribbons of light and rose slowly through the clouds, the atmosphere, through space, and to that realm beyond where the angels waited.

"How are you?" Sara wanted to know.

"I'm all right," God replied.

"So, is the world all finished now?" Moe asked.

"I don't know," God answered. "I don't think so."

"What else are you going to do?" Aviva inquired.

"Me? Nothing."

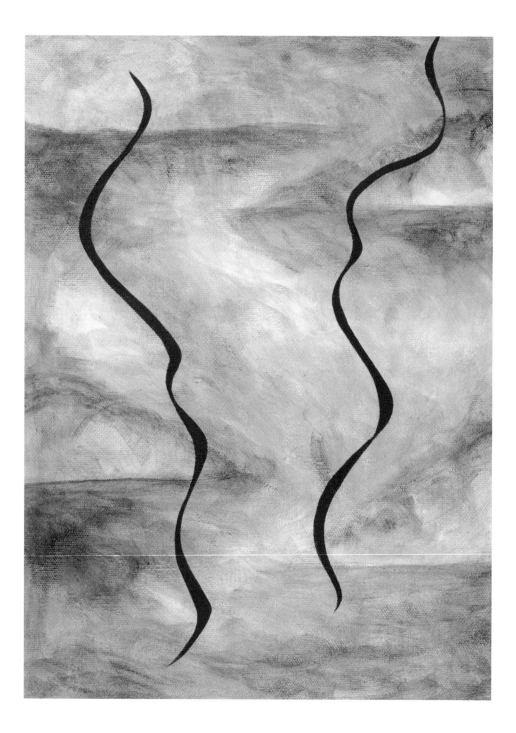

"But you said the world wasn't finished."

"It isn't. Adam and Chavah and all their descendants—they will finish it."

Sara looked down at the world shining in the blackness of space like a jewel. "I wish I were human," she said softly.

"Why?" Moe put in. "You're an angel. Humans die!"

"I know. But they get the chance to finish what God began. Isn't that incredible?"

God hoped people would think so. He dissolved into a golden circle that expanded wider and wider and wider until the universe—even unto infinity—was held within his embrace.

There God remains.

Afterword

In the writing of this book I used a variety of sources. The primary source was my translation from Hebrew of the first three chapters of the book of Genesis. I strove for as literal a translation as possible rather than an interpretive one; that is, I wanted the English to reflect not only literal meanings but the sound, syntax, and structure of Hebrew. Thus I sometimes sacrificed meaning in English to better convey the "feel" of Hebrew. I compared my translation against four others: the King James Version; the Jerusalem Bible; *The Torah: A Modern Commentary,* by W. Gunther Plaut; and *In the Beginning: A New English Rendition of the Book of Genesis,* translated by Everett Fox.

There are two kinds of midrashim—exegetical and aggadic—and they cover more than two thousand years of Jewish history. To oversimplify, exegetical midrashim are sermons or homilies that intellectually explore a verse or story in the Bible. (In the Jewish context, Bible means what Christians call the Old Testament and what Jews also call the Hebrew Scriptures, or Torah, or Tanach.) Aggadic midrashim explore a biblical text through the imagination and story. The classic collection of aggadic midrashim is Louis Ginzberg's seven-volume work, *Legends of the Jews.* (There is a one-volume abridgment called *Legends of the Bible.*)

Midrashim exist in many languages and cultures, and stories from one culture can contradict similar stories from another. In creating my own stories, I reviewed stories contained in other midrashim collections (see bibliography). Midrash was originally an oral tradition and it continues to this day in both oral and written forms. These stories build on and extend that tradition.

Indispensable in writing these stories was my modest knowledge of Hebrew. With the aid of dictionaries and lexicons, I did my own translations of the biblical texts. (The biblical verses prefacing most of the stories are original translations.) It is the Hebrew text, not English translations, that informs my understanding of the creation stories.

Example: English translations say that God created Eve from a rib of Adam's. However, the Hebrew word translated as "rib" is *tzela,* which can also be translated as "side." That is the preferred meaning given by some rabbinic commentators and the one I use here.

These stories do not adhere strictly to the letter of Jewish tradition. However, they are authentic in their affirmation of the faculty of the imagination. Through midrashim Judaism sanctifies the imagination. Example: Some people reading these stories without knowledge of Jewish tradition and Torah might consider too fanciful the portrayal of the Snake in the Garden of Eden as walking upright and speaking. Yet when God curses the Snake, one of the curses is that he will crawl on his belly in the dust. The rabbinic commentators reasoned thus: If his curse was to crawl on his belly, he had to have been walking upright. (I would also like to note that in the Christian tradition, the Snake who persuades Eve to eat the "apple," a fruit not found in the Bible and certainly not in this story, is synonymous with Satan. In the Jewish tradition, some rabbis consider the Snake and Satan to be the same and others do not. Here, the Snake and Satan are not the same, and the Snake does not act as Satan's surrogate in tempting Eve.)

In my retelling of the Adam and Eve story, I have given the story a measure of sensuality with which some parents and teachers might not be comfortable reading to a younger child. My decision to do so was based on the Hebrew in which the sexuality is more explicit and is almost impossible to translate. Anyone reading these stories should feel free to omit whatever he or she is uncomfortable with.

However, my wish is that such passages will be seen as opportunities to discuss sexuality with children. Children are assaulted daily by images of sexuality through advertisements, music videos, and television programs. They are not provided with such images in the context of the sacred. In Judaism, the sacred and the sexual are not regarded as warring opposites but rather the sexual is transformed by the sacred as an offering to the Divine. Thus my intent here.

Sources

GOD BATTLES THE QUEEN OF THE WATERS

Louis Ginzberg's *The Legends of the Jews,* vol. 1, p. 18; Angelo S. Rappoport's *Myth and Legend of Ancient Israel,* p. 14; and *The Book of Legends Sefer Ha-Aggadah: Legends from the Talmud and Midrash,* edited by Hayim Nahman Bialik and Yehoshua Hana Ravnitzky, translated by William G. Braude, p. 10; *Hebrew Myths: The Book of Genesis,* by Robert Graves and Raphael Patai; *Documents from Old Testament Times,* edited by D. Winton Thomas; David N. Freedman's *The Anchor Bible Dictionary,* vol. 2. *Tehom* is a Hebrew word meaning "the deep." Tehom is related to the Babylonian goddess Tiamat, and those familiar with that legend may recognize a similarity in the battle between God and Tehom, and Marduk and Tiamat. Here, however, I have made God feminine, which is a radical archetypal departure. References to Tehom are scattered throughout the Hebrew scriptures, and the basis for Tehom being confined at the bottom of the sea is found in Prov. 8:27–29, where God "put the deeps [*tehomot,* pl.] In storehouses." Interestingly, there are legends which say that when God destroyed the world by water he released Tehom from the bottom of the ocean.

Versions of the second legend of God encircling the waters with sand is found in Ginzberg, *The Midrash on Psalms,* and *The Book of Legends.*

SUN AND MOON

Ginzberg, vol. 1, pp. 23–26; Graves and Patai, p. 36; Rappoport, pp. 14–15; Bialik and Ravnitzky, p. 11.

STRANGE CREATURES

There are many versions of the stories about the creatures, with varied details in each. The sources used here are Ginzberg, vol. 1, pp. 28–34; Rappoport, p. 16; Micha Joseph Bin Gorion's *Mimekor Yisrael: Classical Jewish Folktales,* vol. 1, pp. 5–6.

THE ANGEL OF DEATH

Versions can be found in Bin Gorion, p. 10; and Leo Pavlat's *Jewish Folktales.* Mine is adapted from the version in Ginzberg, vol. 1, pp. 40–42. The names of the angels of death are also taken from Ginzberg, but from vol. 5, p. 57, note 187.

CAT AND MOUSE

Identical versions are found in Ginzberg, vol. 1, p. 35; and Bin Gorion, p. 22.

LEVIATHAN AND FOX

See notes for "The Angel of Death."

CROW LEARNS A LESSON
Pavlat, p. 31; Stern and Mirsky, *Rabbinic Fantasies,* p. 191.

THE GRAND PARADE
Ginzberg, vol. 1, pp. 61–64.

GOD MAKES PEOPLE
Ginzberg, vol. 1, pp. 52–58; vol. 5, pp. 63–78. The details about the five souls are adapted from *Genesis Rabbah,* p. 117. The detail about taking care of the garden was taken from *Ecclesiastes Rabbah,* p. 195, and is also quoted in Bialik and Ravnitzky, pp. 14–15.

GOD CREATES ADAM
Ginzberg, vol. 1, pp. 61–67; Bin Gorion, pp. 6–7; Freedman, p. 135.

GOD CREATES WOMAN
There are many legends about Lilith scattered throughout the Ginzberg volumes. I have reinterpreted the Lilith legend as the projection of evil by men onto women.

ADAM MARRIES
Ginzberg, vol. 1, pp. 64–69.

The line in this story about God making women smarter than men is not so much a feminist interpolation as it is an adaptation of the line from the original legend, which reads that "the intelligence of women matures more quickly than the intelligence of man" (Ginzberg, vol. 1, p. 67).

THE SNAKE
Although this tale draws on traditional sources for its broad outlines and some of its details, the majority of it is original. I refer specifically to the characterizations of Snake and Adam and Eve—characterizations implied in the traditional sources but developed more fully here. The story of Adam and Eve is one I have studied for many years and taught both in synagogues and in my Biblical Tales and Legends course at the University of Massachusetts. Thus, I have done my own translation of the story from Hebrew to English and much of my understanding of the story derives from a Hebrew reading, not a translation. However, the interpretation here is a traditional Jewish one, that is, that there is no original sin, and that the sin was not disobedience but failure to take responsibility. This is directly in line with the Jewish understanding of sin.

For sources used, see Ginzberg, vol 1., pp. 69–83; Ginzberg, vol. 5, pp. 90–110; *Genesis Rabbah,* pp. 148–179; Bialik and Ravnitzky, pp. 20–23.

Bibliography

BOOKS

Abrahams, Roger D., ed. *Afro-American Folktales: Stories from Black Traditions in the New World.* New York: Pantheon Books, 1985.

Bialik, Hayim Nahman, and Yehoshua Hana Ravnitzky. *The Book of Legends Sefer Ha-Aggadah: Legends from the Talmud and Midrash.* Translated by William G. Braude. New York: Schocken Books, 1992. Originally published in Hebrew in Odessa, 1908–1911.

Bin Gorion, Micha Joseph. *Mimekor Yisrael: Classical Jewish Folktales.* Vol. 1. Translated by I. M. Lask. Bloomington, Ind.: Indiana University Press, 1976.

Black, Matthew, ed. *The Book of Enoch, or I Enoch: A New English Edition.* Leiden, the Netherlands: E. J. Brill, 1985.

Charlesworth, James H., ed. *The Old Testament Pseudepigrapha.* Vol. 2. Garden City, N.Y.: Doubleday, 1985.

Fox, Everitt, trans. *In the Beginning: A New English Rendition of the Book of Genesis.* New York: Schocken Books, 1983.

Freedman, Dr. Rabbi H., and Maurice Simon, trans. and eds. *Midrash Rabbah.* 3rd ed. New York: Soncino Press, 1983.

Ginzberg, Louis, ed. *The Legends of the Jews.* Vols. 1–7. Translated by Henrietta Szold. Philadelphia: Jewish Publication Society of America, 1909, 1937.

Graves, Robert, and Raphael Patai. *Hebrew Myths: The Book of Genesis.* New York: 1964.

Pavlat, Leo. *Jewish Folktales.* Translated by Stephen Finn. New York: Greenwich House, 1986.

Plaut, W. Gunther. *The Torah: A Modern Commentary.* New York: Union of American Hebrew Congregations, 1974.

Rappoport, Angelo S. *Myth and Legend of Ancient Israel.* 3 vols. New York: Ktav Publishing, 1966.

Stern, David, and Mark Jay Mirsky. *Rabbinic Fantasies: Imaginative Narratives from Classical Hebrew Literature.* New Haven, Conn.: Yale University Press, 1998.

Thomas, D. Winton, ed. *Documents from Old Testament Times.* New York: HarperCollins, 1961.

CD-ROMS

The Book of Legends. Chicago: Davka Corporation, 1995.

The Soncino Midrash Rabbah. Brooklyn, N.Y.: Davka Corporation, 1995.

The Soncino Talmud. Chicago: Davka Corporation in conjunction with Judaica Press, 1995.